TEXAS
Brides

JOAN JOHNSTON

TEXAS *Brides*

HQN™

HQN™

ISBN 0-373-77042-1

TEXAS BRIDES

CONTENTS

Dear Reader,

I had no idea when I wrote *The Rancher & the Runaway Bride* that I was starting a dynasty that would encompass three generations of Whitelaws in Texas. I grew up in a large family—six girls and one boy—and I always wondered what it might have been like to have older brothers. For heroine Tate Whitelaw, her brothers Garth, Jesse and Faron, turn out to be a little more protective than she would like. When they set boundaries that she finds too constraining, she heads off on an adventure that lands her in trouble—and leads her to her one true love.

I hope you'll enjoy this book in my HAWK'S WAY series, which follows the lives and loves of a powerful and prolific Texas ranching family.

Long after writing *The Bluest Eyes in Texas,* I'm still writing about Texas Rangers and making them my heroes. They're a fascinating, elite breed of modern-day lawmen who remain renegades and lone wolves. Burr Covington is one of my favorites!

I have no trouble picturing "the bluest eyes in Texas" because my heroine's eyes aren't really blue—they're the color of Texas bluebonnets, which are actually a striking lavender. I have pictures of my children playing among those glorious Texas wildflowers, which blanket the hill country in south Texas each spring.

I invite you along as Burr Covington, a Texas Ranger from the wrong side of the tracks, rescues the governor's "ice princess" daughter from kidnappers, and then falls head over heels for *The Bluest Eyes in Texas.*

I love hearing from you! You can contact me through my Web site at www.joanjohnston.com. Be sure to sign up on my mailing list if you'd like to get notice of upcoming titles.

Happy reading!

Joan Johnston

THE RANCHER &
THE RUNAWAY BRIDE

 Chapter 1

"MAY I kiss you good night, Tate?"

"Of course you can, Hank."

"Your brothers—"

"Forget about them! I'm a grown woman. I certainly don't need permission from Faron or Garth to give you a simple little good-night kiss." Tate Whitelaw stepped closer to the tall cowboy and slipped her arms around his neck. The bright light over the front door didn't quite reach to the corner of the railed porch where she was standing with Hank.

Hank took advantage of Tate's invitation, drawing her into his arms behind one of the massive fluted columns that graced the front of the house and aligning their bodies from breast to hip. She was uncomfortably aware of his arousal, since only two layers of denim—her jeans and his—separated their warm flesh. His mouth sought hers, and his tongue thrust inside. It was more than a simple good-night kiss, and Tate suddenly found herself wishing she hadn't been quite so encouraging.

"Hank—" she gasped, pulling her head back and trying to escape his ardor. "I don't think—"

Hank's arms tightened around her, and Tate found herself in a wrestling match. She struggled to get the heels of her hands to his shoulders to push him away. He gripped her short black hair with one hand and angled her face for his kiss.

"Hank! S-stop it!" she hissed.

Caught up in his lust, Hank was oblivious to Tate's urgently whispered entreaties. Tate had already decided it was time to take desperate action when the issue was taken out of her hands. Literally.

Tate knew someone had arrived on the scene when Hank gave a grunt of surprise as he was jerked away from her. Her brother Faron had a handful of Hank's Western shirt in his grasp and was holding the young man at arm's length.

"What the hell do you think you're doing with my sister?" Faron demanded.

Hank blinked owlishly. "Kissing her?"

"Who the hell gave you permission to kiss her?"

"I did!" Tate said through gritted teeth. Fisted hands on hips, chin up, she faced her brother defiantly. "Who gave *you* permission to interfere!"

"When I see my kid sister getting mauled—"

"I can take care of myself!"

Faron arched a brow, and Tate knew it was because she hadn't denied the fact she was being mauled. Hank had just been a little exuberant, that was all. She could have escaped her predicament without her brother's interference.

To Tate's horror, Garth shoved open the front screen door and asked, "What in blue blazes is going on out here?"

"I found this coyote forcing his attentions on Tate," Faron said.

Garth stepped onto the porch, and if the sheer size of him

didn't intimidate, the fierce scowl on his face surely would have. "That true?" Garth demanded of Hank.

Hank gulped. Perspiration dripped at his temple. The color left his face. "Well, sir…" He looked to Tate for rescue.

Tate watched Garth's lips flatten into a grim line as he exchanged a decisive look with Faron. Hank had been tried and convicted. All that was left was sentencing.

"Get your butt out of here," Garth said to Hank. "And don't come back."

Faron gave Hank a pretty good shove in the right direction, and Garth's boot finished the job. Hank stumbled down the porch steps to his pickup, dragged open the door, gunned the engine and departed in a swirl of gravel and choking dust.

There was a moment of awful silence while the dust settled. Tate fought the tears that threatened. She would *never* let her brothers know how humiliated she felt! But there was nothing wrong with giving them the lash of her tongue. She turned and stared first into Garth's stern, deep brown eyes, and then into Faron's more concerned gray-green ones.

"I hope you're both happy!" she snapped. "That's the fourth man in a month you've run off the ranch."

"Now, Tate," Faron began. "Any man who won't stand up to the two of us isn't worth having for a beau."

"Don't patronize me!" she raged. "I won't be placated like a baby with a rattle. I'm not three. I'm not even thirteen. I'm twenty-three. I'm a woman, and I have a woman's needs."

"You don't need to be manhandled," Garth said. "And I won't stand by and let it happen."

"Me neither," Faron said.

Tate hung her head. When she raised it again, her eyes were

glistening with tears that blurred her vision. "I could have handled Hank myself," she said in a quiet voice. "You have to trust me to make my own decisions, my own mistakes."

"We don't want to see you hurt," Faron said, laying a hand on Tate's shoulder.

Tate stiffened. "And you think I wasn't hurt by what happened here tonight?"

Garth and Faron exchanged another look. Then Faron said, "Maybe your pride was pricked a little, but—"

"A *little!*" Tate jerked herself from Faron's grasp. "You're impossible! Both of you! You don't know the first thing about what I want or need. You can't imagine what it's like to have every step you take watched to make sure you don't fall down. Maybe it made sense when I was a baby, but I'm grown-up now. I don't need you standing guard over me."

"Like you didn't need our help tonight?" Garth asked in a cold voice.

"I didn't!" Tate insisted.

Garth grabbed her chin and forced her face up to his. "You have no idea what a man's passions can lead him to do, little sister. I have no intention of letting you find out. Until the right man comes along—"

"There's no man who'll come within a hundred miles of this place now," Tate retorted bitterly. "My loving brothers have seen to that! You're going to keep me a virgin until I dry up and—"

Garth's fingers tightened painfully on her jaw, forcing her to silence. She saw the flash of fury in his dark eyes. A muscle flexed in his jaw. At last he said, "You'd better go to your room and think about what happened here tonight. We'll talk more about this tomorrow."

"You're not my father!" Tate spat. "I won't be sent to my room like a naughty child!"

"You'll go, or I'll take you there," Garth threatened.

"She can't go anywhere until you let go of her chin," Faron pointed out.

Garth shot a rueful look at his brother, then released Tate. "Good night, Tate," he said.

Tate had learned there were only two sides to Garth's arguments: his and the wrong one. Her stomach was churning. Her chest felt so tight it was hard to breathe, and her throat had a lump in it that made swallowing painful. Her eyes burned with tears that she would be *damned* if she'd shed!

She looked from Garth to Faron and back again. Garth's face was a granite mask of disapproval, while Faron's bore a look of sympathetic understanding. Tate knew they loved her. It was hard to fight their good intentions. Yet their love was smothering her. They would not let her *live!*

Her mother had died when she was born, and she had been raised by her father and her three brothers, Garth, Faron and Jesse. Their father had died when Tate was eight. Jesse had left home then, and Garth and Faron had been responsible for her ever since. It was a responsibility they had taken very seriously. She had been kept cloistered at Hawk's Way, more closely guarded than a novice in a convent. If she went anywhere off the ranch, one of her brothers came along.

When Tate was younger she'd had girlfriends to share her troubles with. As she got older, she discovered that the females she met were more interested in getting an introduction to her brothers than in being her friend. Eventually, she had simply stopped inviting them.

Tate hadn't even been allowed to go away to college. Instead she had taken correspondence courses to get her degree in business. She had missed the social interaction with her peers, the experience of being out on her own, that would have prepared her to deal with the Hanks of the world.

However, Garth and Faron had taught her every job that had to be done on a ranch, from branding and castrating to vaccinating and breeding. She wasn't naive. No one could be raised on a ranch and remain totally innocent. She had seen the quarter horse stallions they raised at Hawk's Way mount mares. But she could not translate that violent act into what happened between a man and a woman in bed.

So far, she had found the fumbling kisses of her swains more annoying than anything else. Yet Tate had read enough to know there was more to the male-female relationship than she had experienced so far. If her brothers had their way, she would never unravel the mysteries of love.

She had come to the dire conclusion over the past few months that no man would ever pass muster with her brothers. If she continued living with them, she would die an old maid. They had given her no choice. In order to escape her brothers' overprotectiveness, she would have to leave Hawk's Way.

This latest incident was the final straw. But then, kicking a man when he's down is sometimes the only way to make him get up. Tate took one long, last look at each of her brothers. She would be gone from Hawk's Way before morning.

When the front door closed behind Tate, Faron settled a hip on the porch rail, and Garth leaned his shoulder against the doorjamb.

"She's too damn beautiful for her own good," Garth muttered.

"Hard to believe a woman can look so sexy in a man's T-shirt and a pair of jeans," Faron agreed with a shake of his head.

Garth's eyes were bleak. "What're we going to do about her?"

"Don't know that there's anything we can do except what we're already doing."

"I don't want to see her get hurt," Garth said.

Faron felt a tightness in his chest. "Yeah, I know. But she's all grown up, Garth. We're going to have to let go sometime."

Garth frowned. "Not yet."

"When?"

"I don't know. Just not yet."

THE NEXT MORNING, Garth and Faron met in the kitchen, as they always did, just before dawn. Charlie One Horse, the part-Indian codger who had been chief cook and bottle washer at Hawk's Way since their mother had died, had coffee perking and breakfast on the table. Only this morning there was something—someone—missing.

"Where's Tate?" Garth asked as he sat down at the head of the table.

"Ain't seen her," Charlie said.

Garth grimaced. "I suppose she's sulking in her room."

"You drink your coffee, and I'll go upstairs and check on her," Faron offered.

A moment later Faron came bounding into the kitchen. "She's not there! She's gone!"

Garth sprang up from his chair so fast it fell over backward. "What? Gone where?"

Faron grabbed Garth by the shoulders and said in a fierce voice, "She's not in her room. Her bed hasn't been slept in!"

Garth freed himself and took the stairs two at a time to see for himself. Sure enough, the antique brass double bed was made up with its nubby-weave spread. That alone was an ominous sign. Tate wasn't known for her neatness, and if she had made up the bed, she had done it to make a statement.

Garth headed for the closet, his heart in his throat. He heaved a sigh of relief when he saw Tate's few dresses still hanging there. Surely she wouldn't have left Hawk's Way for good without them.

Garth turned and found Faron standing in the doorway to Tate's room. "She probably spent the night sleeping out somewhere on the ranch. She'll turn up when she gets hungry."

"I'm going looking for her," Faron said.

Garth shoved a hand through his hair, making it stand on end. "Hell and the devil! I guess there'll be no peace around here until we find her. When I get hold of her, I'll—"

"When we find her, I'll do the talking," Faron said. "You've caused enough trouble."

"Me? This isn't my fault!"

"Like hell! You're the one who told her to go to her room and stay there."

"Looks like she didn't pay a whole helluva lot of attention to me, did she?" Garth retorted.

At that moment Charlie arrived, puffing from exertion, and said, "You two gonna go look for that girl, or stand here arguin'?"

Faron and Garth glared at each other for another moment before Faron turned and pressed his way past Charlie and down the stairs.

Charlie put a hand out to stop Garth. "Don't think you're

gonna find her, boy. Knew this was bound to happen sooner or later."

"What do you mean, old man?"

"Knew you had too tight a rein on that little filly. Figured she had too much spirit to stay in them fences you set up to hold her in."

"It was for her own good!"

Charlie shook his head. "Did it as much for yourself as for her. Knowin' your ma like you did, it's no wonder you'd want to keep your sister close. Prob'ly fearful she'd take after your ma, steppin' out on your pa like she did and—"

"Leave Mother out of this. What she did has nothing to do with the way I've treated Tate."

Charlie tightened the beaded rawhide thong that held one of his long braids, but said nothing.

Garth scowled. "I can see there's no sense arguing with a stone wall. I'm going after Tate, and I'm going to bring her back. This time she'll stay put!"

Garth and Faron searched canyons and mesas, ridges and gullies on their northwest Texas ranch, but not a sign did they find of their sister on Hawk's Way.

It was Charlie One Horse who discovered that the old '51 Chevy pickup, the one with the rusty radiator and the skipping carburetor, was missing from the barn where it was stored.

Another check of Tate's room revealed that her underwear drawer was empty, that her brush and comb and toothpaste were gone, and that several of her favorite T-shirts and jeans had also been packed.

By sunset, the truth could not be denied. At the age of twenty-three, Tate Whitelaw had run away from home.

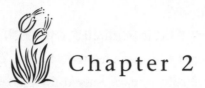

Chapter 2

ADAM PHILIPS NORMALLY DIDN'T stop to pick up hitchhikers. But there was no way he could drive past the woman sitting on the front fender of a '51 Chevy pickup, its hood raised and its radiator steaming, her thumb outstretched to bum a ride. He pulled his late-model truck up behind her and put on his Stetson as he stepped out into the heat of a south Texas midsummer afternoon.

She was wearing form-fitting jeans and an off-the-shoulder peasant blouse that exposed a lush female figure. But the heart-shaped face, with its huge hazel eyes and wide mouth framed by breeze-ruffled, short-cropped black hair, was innocence itself. He was stunned by her beauty and appalled at her youth. What was this female doing all alone on an isolated stretch of southwest Texas highway in an old rattletrap truck?

She beamed a trusting smile at him, and he felt his heart do a flipflop. She slipped off the rusty fender and lazily sauntered toward him. He felt his groin tighten with desire and scowled. She stopped in her tracks. About time she thought to be wary! Adam was all too conscious of the dangers a stranger presented to a young woman alone. Grim-lipped, he strode the short distance between the two vehicles.

Tate had been so relieved to see *someone* show up on the deserted rural route that the danger of the situation didn't immediately occur to her. She got only a glimpse of wavy blond hair and striking blue eyes before her rescuer had slipped on a Stetson that put his face in shadow.

He was broad-shouldered and lean-hipped, with a stride that ate up the distance between the two trucks. It was a fair assumption, from his dusty boots, worn jeans and sweat-stained Western shirt, that he was a working cowboy. Tate saw no reason to suspect he meant her any harm.

But instead of a pleasant "May I help you?" the first words out of his mouth were, "What the hell do you think you're doing?"

Tate was alarmed by the animosity in the stranger's voice and frightened by the intensity of his stare. But his attitude was so similar to what she had recently gone through with her brothers that she lifted her chin and retorted, "Hitching a ride back to the nearest gas station. In case you hadn't noticed, my truck's broken down."

The scowl deepened but he said, "Get in my pickup."

Tate had only taken two steps when the tall cowboy grabbed her arm and pulled her up short.

"Aren't you going to ask anything about me? Don't you want to know who I am?"

By now Tate was more irritated than frightened. "A Good Samaritan with a bad temper!" she retorted. "Do I need to know more?"

Adam opened his mouth to make a retort, took one look at the mutinous expression on the young woman's face, and shut it again. Instead he dragged her unceremoniously to the passenger's side of his long-bed pickup, opened the door, shoved her inside, and slammed it closed after her.

"My bag! It's in the back end of the Chevy," Tate yelped.

Adam stalked back to the rattletrap Chevy, snagged the duffel bag from the rusted-out truck bed and slung it into the back of his pickup.

Woman was too damned trusting for her own good! he thought. Her acid tongue wouldn't have been much help to her if he had been the kind of villain who preyed on stranded women. Which he wasn't. Lucky for her!

Tate didn't consider herself at all lucky. She recognized the flat-lipped expression on her Good Samaritan's face. He might have rescued her, all right, but he wasn't happy about it. The deep crevices formed around his mouth by his frown and the webbed lines at the edges of his eyes had her guessing his age at thirty-five or thirty-six—the same as her eldest brother Garth. The last thing she needed was another keeper!

She sat back with her arms crossed and stared out the window as they drove past rolling prairie. She thought back to the night two weeks ago when she had decided to leave Hawk's Way.

Her escape from her brothers, while apparently sudden, hadn't been completely without direction. She had taken several ranch journals containing advertisements from outfits all over Texas looking for expert help and headed south. However, Tate soon discovered that not one rancher was interested in hiring a woman, especially one without references, as either foreman or ranch manager.

To confound her problems, the ancient pickup she had taken from the barn was in worse shape than she had thought. It had left her stranded miles from the Lazy S—the last ranch on her list and her last hope for a job in ranch management.

"Do you know where the Lazy S is?" she asked.

Adam started at the sound of her voice. "I expect I could find it. Why?"

"I understand they're looking for a ranch manager. I intend to apply for the job."

"You're just a kid!"

The cowboy could have said nothing more likely to raise Tate's neck hairs. "For your information, I'm twenty-three and a fully grown woman!"

Adam couldn't argue with that. He had a pretty good view of the creamy rise of her breasts at the frilly gathered edge of her blouse. "What do you know about ranching?" he asked.

"I was raised on a ranch, Hawk's Way, and—" She stopped abruptly, realizing that she had revealed more than she had intended to this stranger. Tate hadn't used her own last name to apply for any jobs, knowing that if she did her brothers would be able to hunt her down and drag her back home. "I hope you'll keep that to yourself," she said.

Adam raised an inquiring brow that met such a gamine smile that his heart did that disturbing flipflop again.

"You see," Tate said, "the truth is, I've run away from home."

Adam snorted. "Aren't you a little old for that?"

Tate's lips curled ruefully. "I suppose so. But my brothers just wouldn't let me *live!* I mean, they watched every breath in and out of my body."

Adam found the thought rather intriguing himself.

"My brothers are a little overprotective, you see. I had to run away if I was ever going to meet the right man and fall in love and have children."

"Sounds like you could do that better at home than traipsing around the countryside," Adam observed.

"You don't know my older brothers! They want to wrap me in cotton batting and keep me safe. Safe, ha! What they mean is, they want to keep me a virgin forever."

Adam choked at this unbelievable revelation and coughed to clear his throat.

"It's true! They've chased away every single beau I've ever had. Which is only a waste of time and energy because, you know, a man who's born to drown can manage to drown in a desert."

Adam eyed her askance.

"I mean, if something is destined to happen, it'll happen no matter what."

Tate waited for Adam to say something, but when he remained silent, she continued, "My older brother, Jesse, left home, too, when I was just eight. It was right after my father died. We haven't seen him for years and years. I don't plan to stay away for years, of course, but then, who knows how long it will take to find my Prince Charming. Not that I have to marry a prince of a man."

Tate grinned and shrugged. "But it would be nice, you know, to just once kiss a man good night, without having my brothers send him packing because he's not good enough for me."

Tate realized she was talking to fill the silence and forced herself to shut up.

Behind the young woman's bravado Adam saw the desperation that had sent her fleeing from the safe haven her brothers had provided for her. He felt sick inside. Was this the way his younger sister had felt? Had Melanie seen him as an oppressive tyrant, the same way this young woman perceived her brothers?

Tate held her breath as the stranger looked into her eyes. There was an awful sadness there she felt constrained to dispel. So she began talking again.

"I've been looking everywhere for a job," she said. "I must have been to fifteen different spreads in the past two weeks. But I haven't had so much as a nibble of interest.

"What I find so frustrating is the fact that most owners don't treat me seriously. I mean, I know I'm young, but there isn't anything I don't know about running a ranch."

"Do you know how to figure the amount of feed you need for each head of stock?" Adam asked.

"Depends on whether you plan to keep the stock penned or let it graze," Tate said. "Now if it's penned—"

Adam interrupted with, "Give me some symptoms of colic."

"A horse might have colic if he won't eat, or if he starts pawing, or gets up and down a lot. Generally an animal that can't get comfortable has a problem."

"Can you keep books on a computer?"

Tate snorted inelegantly. "Boy can I ever! I got stuck with all the bookkeeping at Hawk's Way. So, if you were hiring at the Lazy S, would I get the job?"

"What will you do if you *don't* get the job?" Adam asked instead.

Tate shrugged, not realizing how revealing the gesture was of the fact she wasn't the least bit nonchalant about that distressing possibility. "I don't know. I only know I *won't* go back home."

"And if your brothers find you?"

Her chin took on a mulish tilt. "I'll just run away again."

Adam wondered if his sister was so forthright and disarmingly honest with the man who had picked her up the night she ran away from home. Had that stranger known all about the young woman he had raped and murdered and left lying in a ditch on the side of the road?

Adam's teeth clenched in determination. If he had anything to say about it, the innocent young woman in his pickup would not become another such statistic. And he, of all people, was in a perfect position to help her. Because he owned the Lazy S Ranch.

However, in the months since Adam had put his advertisement in the ranch journal, he had changed his mind about needing a foreman. He had decided to place his country medical practice on hold and put the Lazy S Ranch back in the black himself.

But if he told this young woman he had no job for her, where would she go? What would she do? And how would he feel if he sent her away and she ended up dead somewhere on the side of the road?

"Say, there's the Lazy S Ranch!" Tate pointed at a wrought-iron sign that bridged a dirt road off the main thoroughfare. To her surprise, the cowboy turned and drove across a cattle guard onto the Lazy S.

"I thought you were going to take me into town!" she said.

"I thought you wanted to interview for a job!" he retorted.

Tate eyed the cowboy. She was perplexed. Many western men were the strong, silent type, but the stranger who had picked her up was something more. Aloof. The more distant he was, the more intrigued she became. It was a surprise to find out he had been kind enough to take her directly to the Lazy S.

She could have kicked herself for telling him so much personal information without finding out anything about him—not even his name. When he dropped her off, she might never see him again. Tate suddenly realized she wanted to see him again. Very much.

As the cowboy stopped his pickup in front of an impressive adobe ranch house, she said, "I can't tell you how much I appreciate your giving me a ride here. I'd like to thank you, but I don't even know your name!"

Adam turned to look at her and felt a tightening in his gut as she smiled up at him. Well, it was now or never. "My name is Adam Phillips," he said. "I own the Lazy S. Come on inside, and you can interview for that job."

 Chapter 3

Tate was stunned when the mysterious cowboy revealed his identity, but buoyant with hope, as well. She scrambled out of the pickup after Adam, certain that he wouldn't have bothered bringing her here if he didn't intend to at least consider her for the job of ranch foreman.

"Follow me," he said, heading into the house.

Tate stopped only long enough to grab her duffel bag and sling it over her shoulder before scampering up the three steps after him.

Adam's living room was masculine through and through, filled with massive Spanish furniture of natural leather studded with brass. There was not another frill or a furbelow to soften the room. *No woman has lived here in a long time—if ever,* Tate decided.

She discovered that the adobe hacienda formed a U shape. The two wings enclosed a garden shaded by immense moss-laden live oaks and bright with blooming bougainvillea. A central tile fountain splashed with cascading water.

They finally arrived at Adam's office, which was located at the tip of one wing of the house. The thick adobe walls and the barrel-tile roof kept the inside of the house dark and cool, reminiscent of days gone by when everyone took an afternoon siesta.

Tate saw from the immaculate condition of the office that Adam must be an organized person. Everything had a place and everything was in its place. Tate felt her heart sink. She wasn't averse to order, she just refused to be bound by it. That had been one small rebellion she was capable of in the space in which her brothers confined her.

Instead of sitting on the leather chair in front of the desk, she seated herself on a corner of the antique oak desk itself. Adam refused to sit at all, instead pacing the room like a caged tiger.

"Before we go any further, I want to know your real name," he said.

Tate frowned. "I need a promise from you first that you won't contact my brothers."

Adam stopped pacing and stared at her.

Tate stared right back.

"All right," he said. "You've got it."

Tate took a deep breath and said, "My last name is Whitelaw."

Adam swore under his breath and began pacing again. The Whitelaws were known all over Texas for the excellent quarter horses they bred and trained. He had once met Garth Whitelaw at a quarter horse sale. And he was intimately acquainted with Jesse Whitelaw. Tate's brother Jesse, the one she hadn't seen in years, had recently married Honey Farrell—the woman Adam loved.

Honey's ranch, the Flying Diamond, bordered the Lazy S. Fortunately, with the strained relations between Adam and

Jesse Whitelaw, Tate's brother wasn't likely to be visiting the Lazy S anytime soon.

Adam turned his attention to the young woman he had rescued from the side of the road. Her short black hair was windblown around her face, and her cheeks were flushed with excitement. She was gnawing worriedly on her lower lip—something he thought he might like to do himself.

Adam felt that telltale tightening in his groin. He tucked his thumbs into his jeans to keep from reaching out to touch her.

Tate crossed her legs and clutched her knee with laced fingers. She could feel the tension in Adam. A muscle worked in his jaw, and his expression was forbidding. A shiver ran down her spine. But it wasn't fear she felt, it was anticipation.

She was so nervous her voice cracked when she tried to speak. She cleared her throat and asked, "So, do I get the job?"

"I haven't made up my mind yet."

Tate was on her feet and at Adam's side in an instant. "I'd be good at it," she argued. "You wouldn't be sorry you hired me."

Adam had his doubts about that. His blood thrummed as he caught the faint scent of lilacs from her hair. He was already sorry he had stopped to pick her up. He couldn't be anywhere near her without feeling as randy as a teenager. That was a fine state of affairs when he had appointed himself her guardian in her brothers' stead. But he believed Tate when she had said she would just run away again if her brothers tried taking her home. Surely she would be better off here where he could keep a close eye on her.

He carefully stepped away from her and went around to sit behind his desk. Perhaps it would provide a more comfortable barrier between himself and the uncontrollable urges that struck him when he got within touching distance of this engaging runaway.

He steepled his fingers and said, "The job I have available isn't the same one that was advertised."

She braced her palms on the desk and leaned toward him. "Oh? Why not?"

Adam took one look at what her careless posture in the peasant blouse revealed and forced his gaze upward to her wide hazel eyes. "It's complicated."

"How?"

Why didn't she move? He had the irresistible urge to reach out and— He jumped up from behind his desk and started pacing again. "You'd have to know a little bit about what's happened on the Lazy S over the past couple of months."

Tate draped herself sideways across the chair in front of the desk, one leg swinging to release the tension, and said, "I'm listening."

"My previous ranch manager was a crook. He's in prison now, but besides stealing other people's cattle, he embezzled from me. He left my affairs in a mess. Originally, I'd intended to hire someone else to try to straighten things out. Lately I've decided to put my medical practice on hold—"

"Wait a minute!"

Tate sat up and her feet dropped to the floor, depriving Adam of the delicious view he'd had of her derriere.

"Do you mean to tell me you're a doctor?" she asked incredulously.

He shrugged sheepishly. "Afraid so. Over the past few months I've been transferring my practice to another physician who's moved into the area, Dr. Susan Kowalski. Now I have time to supervise the work on the Lazy S myself. What

I really need is someone I can trust to organize the paperwork and do the bookkeeping."

Adam pointed to the computer on a stand near his desk. "That thing and I don't get along. I can't pay much," Adam admitted, "but the job includes room and board." That would keep her from sleeping in her truck, which was about all Adam suspected she could afford right now.

Tate wrinkled her nose. She had cut her teeth on the computer at Hawk's Way, and what she didn't know about bookkeeping hadn't been discovered. But it was the kind of work she liked least of everything she'd done at Hawk's Way. Still, a job was a job. And this was the best offer she had gotten.

"All right. I accept."

Tate stood and held a hand out to Adam to shake on the deal.

When Adam touched her flesh he was appalled by the electricity that streaked between them. He had suspected his attraction to Tate, all the while warning himself not to get involved. His powerful, instantaneous reaction to her still caught him by surprise. He blamed it on the fact that it had been too damn long since he'd had a woman. There were plenty who would willingly satisfy his needs, women who knew the score.

He absolutely, positively, was not going to get involved with a twenty-three-year-old virgin. Especially not some virgin who wanted a husband and a family. For Adam Philips wouldn't give her one—and couldn't give her the other.

Tate was astonished by the jolt she received simply from the clasp of Adam's hand. She looked up into his blue eyes and saw a flash of desire quickly banked. She jerked her hand away, said, "I'm sure we're both going to enjoy this relationship," then flushed at the more intimate interpretation that could be put on her words.

Adam's lips curled in a cynical smile. She was a lamb, all right, and a wily old wolf like himself would be smart to keep his distance. He didn't intend to tell her brothers where she was. But he was betting that sooner or later word of her presence on the Lazy S would leak out, and they would find her. When they did, all hell was going to break loose.

Adam shook his head when he thought of what he was getting himself into. Tate Whitelaw was Trouble with a capital *T.*

"Where do I bunk in?" Tate asked.

Adam dragged his Stetson off and ruffled his blond hair where the sweat had matted it down. He hadn't thought about where he would put her. His previous foreman had occupied a separate room at one end of the bunkhouse. That obviously wouldn't do for Tate.

"I suppose you'll have to stay here in the house," he said. "There's a guest bedroom in the other wing. Come along and I'll show you where it is."

He walked her back through the house, describing the layout of things as they went along. "My bedroom is next to the office. The living room, family room and kitchen are in the center of the house. The last bedroom down the hall on this other wing was set up for medical emergencies, and I haven't had time to refurnish it. The first bedroom on this wing will be your room."

Adam opened the door to a room that had a distinctively southwestern flavor. The furniture was antique Americana, with woven rugs on the floor, a rocker, a dry sink, a wardrobe and a large maple four-poster covered with a brightly patterned quilt. The room felt light and airy. That image was helped by the large sliding glass door that opened onto the courtyard.

Tate sat down on the bed and bounced a couple of times. "Feels plenty comfortable." She turned and smiled her thanks up at Adam.

The smile froze on her face.

His look was avid, his nostrils flared. She was suddenly aware of the softness of the bed. The fact that they were alone. And that she didn't know Adam Philips...from Adam.

However, the part of Tate that was alive to the danger of the situation was squelched by the part of her that was exhilarated to discover she could have such a profound effect on this man. Adam was quite unlike the men her brothers had so peremptorily ejected from Hawk's Way. In some way she could not explain, he was different. She knew instinctively that his kiss, his touch, would be unlike anything she had ever experienced.

Nor did she feel the same person when she was near him. With this man, she was different. She was no longer her brothers' little sister. She was a woman, with a woman's need to be loved by one special man.

Instead of scooting quickly off the bed, she stayed right where she was. She tried her feminine wings just a bit by languidly turning on her side and propping her head up with her hand. She pulled one leg up slightly, mimicking the sexy poses she had seen in some of her brothers' magazines—the ones they thought she knew nothing about.

Adam's reaction was everything she could have wished for. His whole body tautened. A vein in his temple throbbed. The muscles in his throat worked spasmodically. And something else happened. Something which, considering the level she was lying at, she couldn't help observing.

It was fascinating. She had never actually watched it happen to a man before. Mostly, the men she had dated were already in that condition before she had an opportunity to notice. The changing shape of Adam's Levi's left no doubt that he was becoming undeniably, indisputably, absolutely, completely *aroused*.

She gasped, and her eyes sought out his face to see what he intended to do about it.

Nothing! Adam thought. *He was going to do absolutely nothing about the fact this hoyden in blue jeans had him harder than a rock in his crotch.*

"If you're done testing your feminine wiles, I'd like to finish showing you the house," Adam said.

Humiliated by the sarcasm in his voice, Tate quickly scooted off the bed. She had no trouble recognizing his feelings now. Irritation. Frustration. She felt the same things herself. She had never imagined how powerful desire could be. It was a lesson she wouldn't forget.

She stood before him, chin high, unwilling to admit blame or shame or regret for what she had done. "I'm ready."

Then strip down and get into that bed.

Adam clenched his teeth to keep from saying what he was thinking. He didn't know when he had felt such unbridled lust for a woman. It wasn't decent. But he damn sure wasn't going to do anything about it!

"Come on," he growled. "Follow me."

Tate followed Adam back through the house to the kitchen, where they found a short, rotund Mexican woman with snapping black eyes and round, rosy cheeks. She was chopping onions at the counter. Tate was treated to a smile that revealed two rows of brilliant white teeth.

"Who have you brought to meet me, Señor Adam?" the woman asked.

"Maria, this is Tate Whitelaw. She's going to be my new bookkeeper. Tate will be staying in the guest bedroom. Tate, I'd like you to meet my housekeeper, Maria Fuentes."

"*Buenos días, Maria,*" Tate said.

"*¡Habla usted español?*" Maria asked.

"You've already heard all I know," Tate said with a self-deprecating grin.

Maria turned to Adam and said in Spanish, "She is very pretty, this one. And very young. Perhaps you would wish me to be her *dueña*."

Adam flushed and answered in Spanish, "I'm well aware of her age, Maria. She doesn't need a chaperon around me."

The Mexican woman arched a disbelieving brow. Again in Spanish she said, "You are a man, Señor Adam. And her eyes, they smile at you. It would be hard for any man to refuse such an invitation. No?"

"No!" Adam retorted. Then added in Spanish, "I mean, no I wouldn't take advantage of her. She has no idea what she's saying with her eyes."

Maria's disbelieving brow arched higher. "If you say so, Señor Adam."

Tate had been trying to follow the Spanish conversation, but the only words she recognized were "Maria," "chaperon," "Señor Adam" and "No." The look on Maria's face made it clear she disapproved of the fact Tate would be living in the house alone with Adam. Well, she didn't need a chaperon any more than she needed a keeper. She could take care of herself.

Fortunately, it wasn't necessary for her to interrupt the conversation. A knock at the kitchen door did it for her. The door opened before anyone could answer it, and a young cowhand stuck his head inside. He had brown eyes and auburn hair and a face so tanned it looked like rawhide.

"Adam? You're needed in the barn to take a look at that mare, Break of Day. She's having some trouble foaling."

"Sure. I'll be there in a minute, Buck."

Instead of leaving, the cowhand stood where he was, his eyes glued on the vision in a peasant blouse and skin tight jeans standing in Adam's kitchen. He stepped inside the door, slipped his hat off his head, and said, "Name's Buck, ma'am."

Tate smiled and held out her hand. "Tate Wh—atly."

The cowboy shook her hand and then stood there foolishly grinning at her.

Adam groaned inwardly. This was a complication he should have foreseen, but hadn't. Tate was bound to charm every cowhand on the place. He quickly crossed past her and put a hand on Buck's shoulder to urge him out the door. "Let's go."

"Can I come with you?" Tate asked.

Before Adam could say no, Buck spoke up.

"Why sure, ma'am," the cowboy said. "Be glad to have you along."

There wasn't much Adam could say except, "You can come. But stay out of the way."

"What kind of trouble is the mare having?" Adam asked as they crossed the short distance to the barn, Tate following on their heels.

"She's down and her breathing's labored," Buck said.

Tate saw as soon as they entered the stall that the mare was indeed in trouble. Her features were grim as she settled onto the straw beside the mare's head. "There now, pretty lady. I know it's hard. Just relax, you pretty lady, and everything will be all right."

Adam and Buck exchanged a look of surprise and approval at the calm, matter-of-fact way Tate had insinuated herself with the mare. The mare lifted her head and whickered in response to the sound of Tate's voice. Then she lay back down and a long, low groan escaped her.

Tate held the mare's head while Adam examined her. "It's twins."

"Why that's wonderful!" Tate exclaimed.

"One of them's turned wrong, blocking the birth canal." In fact, there was one hoof from each of the twins showing.

"Surely your vet can deliver them!"

Adam's features were somber as he answered, "He's out of town at his daughter's wedding." Adam couldn't imagine a way to save either foal, entangled as they were.

Tate's excitement vanished to be replaced with foreboding. She had encountered this problem once before, and the result had come close to being disastrous. Garth had managed to save the mare and both foals, but it had been a very near thing.

"I'll have to take one foal to save the other," Adam said in a flat voice.

"You mean, destroy it?" Tate asked. She couldn't bring herself to say "dismember it" though that was what Adam was suggesting.

"There's nothing else I can do." Adam turned to the cowboy and said, "Buck, see if you can find me some rope."

Tate stroked the mare's neck, trying to keep the animal calm. She looked up and saw the dread in Adam's eyes. It was never easy to make such decisions, yet they were a constant part of ranch life.

She was hesitant to interfere, but there was the tiniest chance the second foal could be saved. "My brother Garth went through this not too long ago. He was able to save both foals by—"

Buck arrived and interrupted with, "Here's the rope, Adam. Do you need my help?"

"I'm not sure. I'd appreciate it if you'd stay."

Buck propped a foot on the edge of the stall and leaned his arms across the top rail to watch as Adam knelt beside the mare and began to fashion a noose with the rope.

Adam paused and glanced over at Tate. She was gnawing on her lower lip again while she smoothed her hand over the mare's sleek neck.

Adam found himself saying, "If you know something that can be done to save both foals, I'm willing to give it a try."

He watched Tate's whole face light up.

"Yes! Yes, I do." She quickly explained how Garth had re-positioned the foals.

"I'm not sure I—"

"You can do it!" Tate encouraged. "I know you can!"

Her glowing look made him think he might be able to move mountains. As for saving two spindly foals… It was at least worth a try.

A half hour later, sweat had made damp patches under the arms and down the back of Adam's chambray shirt. He had paused in what he was doing long enough to tie a navy blue bandanna around his forehead to keep the salty wetness out of his eyes. He worked quietly, efficiently, aware of the life-and-death nature of his task.

Adam knew a moment of hope when he finished. But now that the foals had been rearranged, the mare seemed too exhausted to push. He looked across the mare to Tate, feeling his failure in every inch of his body. "I'm sorry."

Tate didn't hear his apology. She took the mare's head onto her lap and began chanting and cooing to the exhausted animal—witchcraft for sure, Adam thought—until the mare amazingly, miraculously birthed the first of the foals.

Adam knew his grin had to be as silly as the one on Tate's face, but he didn't care. Buck took care of cleaning up the first foal while Tate continued her incantations until the mare had delivered the second. Buck again took over drying off the foal while Tate remained at the mare's head, and Adam made sure the afterbirths were taken care of.

When Adam was finished, he crossed to a sink at one end of the barn and scrubbed himself clean. He dried his hands with a towel before rolling his sleeves down from above the elbow to the middle of his forearms.

Adam watched in admiration as Tate coaxed the mare onto her feet and introduced her to her offspring. The mare took a tentative lick of one, and then the other. In a matter of minutes both foals were nudging under her belly to find mother's milk.

Tate's eyes met Adam's across the stall. He opened his arms and she walked right into them. Her arms circled his waist, and she held him tightly as she gave vent to the tears she hadn't shed during the awful ordeal.

"Everything's fine, sweetheart. Thanks to you, everything's

just fine," Adam said, stroking her short, silky hair. "Don't cry, sweetheart. You did just fine."

Adam wasn't sure how long they stood there. When he looked up to tell Buck he could go, he discovered the cowboy was already gone. Tate's sobs had subsided and he became aware for the first time of the lithe figure that was pressed so intimately against him.

Tate Whitelaw might be young, but she had the body of a woman. He could feel the soft roundness of her breasts against his chest, and her feminine hips were fitted tight against his masculinity. His growing masculinity.

He tried shifting himself away, but her nose buried itself more deeply at his shoulder and she snuggled closer.

"Tate." He didn't recognize the voice as his own. He cleared his throat and tried again. "Tate."

"Hmm?"

If she didn't recognize the potential danger of the situation was he honor bound to point it out to her? She felt so good in his arms!

Before he could stop himself, his hands had tangled in her hair. He tugged and her head fell back. Her eyes were limpid pools of gold and green. Her face was flushed from crying. She had been gnawing on that lip again and it was swollen. He could see it needed soothing.

He lowered his head and caught her lower lip between his teeth, letting his tongue ride the length of it, testing the fullness of it.

Tate moaned and he was lost.

His tongue slipped into her mouth, tasting her, seeking solace for a desolation of spirit he had never admitted even to himself. Her whole body melted against him, and he was aware of an excruciatingly pleasurable heat in his groin where their bodies were fitted together. He spread his legs slightly and pulled her hard against him, then rubbed them together, creating a friction that turned molten coals to fire.

Tate was only aware of sensations. The softness of his lips. The slickness of his tongue. The heat and hardness of his body pressed tightly against hers. The surge of pleasure as his maleness sought out her femaleness. The urgency of his mouth as it found the smooth column of her neck and teased its way up to her ear, where his breath, hot and moist, made her shiver.

"Please, Adam," she gasped. "Please, don't stop."

Adam's head jerked up, and he stared at the woman in his arms. Good Lord in Heaven! What was he doing?

Adam had to reach behind him to free Tate's arms. He held her at arm's length, his hands gripping hers so tightly he saw her wince. He loosened his hold slightly, but didn't let go. If he did, he was liable to pull her back into his arms and finish what he had started.

Her eyes were lambent, her face rosy with the heat of passion. Her body was languid, boneless with desire, and it wouldn't take much to have her flat on her back beneath him.

Are you out of your mind? What's gotten into you? You're supposed to be protecting her from lechers, not seducing her yourself!

Tate could see Adam was distraught, but she hadn't the least notion why. "What's wrong?" she asked.

Her voice was still breathless and sounded sexy as hell! His body throbbed with need.

"I'll tell you what's wrong, *little girl!*" he retorted. "You may be hotter than a firecracker on the Fourth of July, but I'm not interested in initiating any virgins! Do you hear me? *Flat not interested!*"

"Could have fooled me!" Tate shot back.

Adam realized he was still holding her hands—was in fact rubbing his thumbs along her palms—and dropped them like hot potatoes. "You stay away from me, *little girl*. You're here for one reason, and one reason only—keeping books. You got that?"

"I got it, *big boy!*"

Adam started to reach for her but caught himself. He stalked over and let himself out of the stall. A moment later he was gone from the barn.

Tate shored her arms protectively around herself. What had happened to change things so quickly? One minute Adam had been making sweet, sweet love to her. The next he had become a raving lunatic. Oh, how it had stung when he called her *little girl!* She might be small in stature, but she was all grown up in every way that mattered.

Except for being a virgin.

Tate had to admit she was a babe in the woods when it came to sexual experience. But she recognized that what had just happened between her and Adam was something special. He had wanted her as much as she had wanted him. She couldn't be mistaken about that. But their attraction had been more than sexual. It was as though when she walked into his arms she had found a missing part of herself. And though Adam might discount what had happened because she was so young, she wasn't going to let him get away with denying what had happened between them—to her or to himself.

She wasn't some *little girl* he could dismiss with a wave of his hand. Powerful forces were at work between them. Tate had to find a way to make Adam see her as a woman worthy of his love. But how best to accomplish that goal?

Because the physical attraction between them was so powerful, Tate decided she would start with that. She would put temptation in Adam's path and just see what happened.

Chapter 4

Adam watched Tate smiling up at the cowboys who surrounded her at the corral while she regaled them with another of her outrageous stories about life at Hawk's Way, as she had often done over the past three weeks. As usual, she was dressed in jeans, boots and a T-shirt with some equally outrageous slogan written on it.

Only this T-shirt had the neckline cut out so it slipped down to reveal one shoulder—and the obvious fact that she wasn't wearing a bra. Anyone with eyes in his head could see she was naked under the T-shirt. The three cowboys were sure as hell looking. The wind was blowing and the cotton clung to her, outlining her generous breasts.

Adam told himself he wasn't going to make a fool out of himself by going over there and dragging her away from three sets of ogling male eyes. However, once his footsteps headed in that direction, he didn't seem to be able to stop them.

He arrived in time to hear her say, "My brothers taught me how to get even when some rabbit-shy horse bucks me off."

"How's that, Tate?" one of the cowboys asked.

"Why, I just make that horse walk back to the barn all by himself!" Tate said with a grin.

The cowboys guffawed, and Tate joined in. Adam caught his lip curling with laughter and straightened it back out.

"Don't you have some work to do?" he demanded of the three cowboys.

"Sure, Boss."

"Yeah, Boss."

"Just leaving, Boss."

They tipped their hats to Tate, but continued staring at her as they backed away.

Adam swore acidly, and they quickly turned tail and scattered in three different directions.

He directed a cool stare at Tate and said, "I thought I told you to stay away from my cowhands."

"I believe your exact words were, 'Finish your work before you go traipsing around the ranch,'" Tate replied in a drawl guaranteed to irritate her already irritated boss.

"Is your work done?"

"Had you been home for lunch, I'd have offered to show you the bookkeeping system I've set up. Everything's been logged in and all the current invoices have been paid. I have some suggestions for ways—"

He interrupted with, "What the hell are you doing out here half-dressed, carousing with the hired help?"

"*Carousing?* I was just *talking* to them!" Tate flashed back.

"I want you to leave those boys alone."

"Boys? They looked like grown men to me. Certainly old enough to make up their minds whether or not they want to spend time with me."

Adam grabbed the hat off his head and slapped it against his thigh. "Dammit, Tate. You're a babe in the woods! You're playing with fire, and you're going to get burned! You can't run around here half naked and not expect—"

"Half naked?" she scoffed. "You've got to be kidding!"

"That T-shirt doesn't leave much to the imagination! I can see your nipples plain as day."

Tate looked down and realized for the first time that twin peaks were clearly visible beneath the T-shirt. She decided to brazen it out. "So what if you can? I assume you're familiar with the female anatomy. Besides, you're not my father or my brother. You have absolutely no right to tell me what to wear!"

Since the erotic feelings Adam was experiencing at the moment weren't the least fatherly or brotherly, he didn't argue with her. However, he had appointed himself her guardian in their stead. As such, he felt it his duty to point out to her the dangers of such provocative attire.

He explained in a reasonable voice, "When a man sees a woman looking like that, he just naturally gets ideas."

Tate looked sharply at Adam. "What kind of ideas?"

"The *wrong* kind," Adam said emphatically.

Tate smiled impishly and batted her lashes at him. "I thought you were 'flat not interested' in li'l ole me."

"Cut it out, Tate."

"Cut what out?"

"Stop batting those lashes at me, for one thing."

Tate pouted her lips like a child whose candy had been taken away. "You mean it isn't working?"

It was working all right. Too damn well. She was just precocious enough to be charming. He was entranced despite his wish not to be. He felt his body begin to harden as she slid her gaze from his eyes, to his mouth, to his chest, and straight on down his body to his crotch. Which was putting on a pretty damn good show for her.

"You're asking for it," he said through clenched teeth.

She batted her eyelashes and said, "Am I going to get it?"

"That's it!"

The next thing Tate knew she had been hefted over Adam's shoulder like a sack of wheat, and he was striding toward the house.

"Let me down!" she cried. "Adam, this is uncomfortable."

"Serves you right! You haven't been the least worried about my comfort for the past three weeks."

"Where are you taking me? What are you planning to do with me?"

"Something I'm going to enjoy very much!"

Was Adam really going to make love to her? Would he be rough, or gentle? How was she supposed to act? Was there some sort of proper etiquette for the ravishing of virgins? Not that she had ever worried too much about what was proper. But she felt nervous, anxious about the encounter to come. Finally, Adam would have to acknowledge that greater forces were at work between them than either of them could—or should—resist.

The air inside the adobe house hit her like a cooling zephyr. The dimness left her blind for an instant. Just as she was regaining her sight, they emerged once more into sunlight and she was blinded again. Several more strides and she felt herself being lowered from Adam's shoulder.

Tate barely had time to register the fact that they were in the courtyard when Adam shifted her crosswise in his arms.

Grinning down into her face, he said "Maybe this will cool you off!" and unceremoniously dumped her into the pool of water that surrounded the fountain.

Tate came up spluttering. "Why you!" She blinked her eyes furiously, trying to clear the water from them.

"Why, Miss Tate, are you batting your eyelashes at me again? Guess I'll have to try another dunking."

He took one step toward her, and Tate retreated to the other side of the fountain. "I'll get you for this, you rogue! You roué!"

Adam laughed. It had been so long since he had done so, that the sound brought Maria to the kitchen window to see what Señor Adam found so funny. She shook her head and clucked when she saw the new bookkeeper standing dripping in the fountain. She grabbed a bath towel from the stack of laundry she was folding on the kitchen table and hurried outside with it.

She handed it to Adam and said in Spanish, "This is no way to treat a young woman."

Adam's eyes crinkled at the corners with laughter. "It is when she's bent on seducing an older man."

Maria hissed in a breath and turned to eye the bedraggled creature in the pool. So that was the way the wind was blowing. Well, she was not one to stand in the way of any woman who could make Señor Adam laugh once more.

"Be sure you get the *señorita* dried off quickly. Otherwise she might catch a cold."

Maria left Adam standing with the towel in his hand and a smug grin on his face.

Once the housekeeper was gone, Adam turned back to Tate. And quickly lost his smirk. Because if the T-shirt had been revealing before, it was perfectly indecent now. He could easily see Tate's flesh through the soaked cotton. The cold water had caused her nipples to peak into tight buds.

His mouth felt dry. His voice was ragged as he said, "Here. Wrap yourself in this."

Only he didn't extend the towel to her. He held it so she would have to step out of the pool and into his arms. When he encircled her with the terry cloth she shivered and snuggled closer.

"I'm freezing!" she said.

He, on the other hand, was burning up. How did she do it to him? This time, however, he had only himself to blame. He felt her cold nose burrow into his shoulder as his chin nuzzled her damp hair. The water had released the lilac scent of her shampoo. He took a deep breath and realized he didn't want to let her go.

Adam vigorously rubbed the towel up and down Tate's back, hoping to dispel the intimacy of the moment.

"Mmm. That feels good," she murmured.

His body betrayed him again, responding with amazing rapidity to the throaty sound of her voice. He edged himself away from her, unwilling to admit his need to her. In fact, he felt the distinct necessity to deny it.

"I'm not going to make love to you, Tate."

She froze in his arms. Her head lifted from his shoulder, and he found himself looking into eyes that warmed him like brandy.

"Why not, Adam? Is it because I'm not attractive to you?"

"Lord, no! Of course you're a beautiful woman, but—" Adam groaned as he realized what he had just admitted.

"I am?"

What had those brothers of hers been telling her, Adam wondered, *to make her doubt herself like this?*

"Is it because I don't dress like a lady?"

His only objection to the clothes she wore was his reaction to her in them. "Contrary to what you might have heard, clothes *don't* make the man—or the woman."

"Then it must be the fact that I'm a virgin," she said.

Adam felt himself flushing. "Tate, you just don't go around talking about things like that."

"Not even with you?"

"*Especially* not with me!"

"Why not?"

They were back to that again. He turned her so he had an arm around her shoulder, and began ushering her across the courtyard to her bedroom. "I think it's time you got out of those wet clothes."

Tate's impish smile reappeared. "Would you like to help me?"

"Not on your life!" He opened the sliding glass door and gave her a nudge inside. "I'll meet you in the office in fifteen minutes and you can show me whatever bookkeeping wonders you've accomplished today." He turned and marched across the courtyard, fighting the urge to look back.

Once she was alone in her room, Tate let the towel drop. She stared at herself in the standing oval mirror in the corner and groaned. She looked like something the cat had dragged in! No wonder Adam hadn't been interested!

Tate sat down on a wooden chair to pull off her wet boots, then yanked her T-shirt off and struggled with the wet zipper of her jeans. She peeled her silk panties down and quickly began replacing her clothing with an identical wardrobe. All except the wet boots, for which she substituted a pair of beaded Indian moccasins Charlie One Horse had given her for Christmas.

While Tate dressed, she reviewed the events of the past three weeks since she had arrived at the Lazy S. Teasing Adam had begun as a way of making him admit the sexual attraction—and something more—that existed between them. But she had discovered that kidding some folks was like teasing a loaded polecat. The satisfaction was short-lived.

Tate hadn't been enjoying the game much these days, mainly because she had begun to suffer from the sexually charged situations as much as Adam. The problem was, on her side at least, her heart followed where her hormones led.

She would give anything if Adam was as interested in her as Buck seemed to be. The lean-hipped cowboy had been asking her every day for a week if she would go out with him on Saturday night. Well, maybe she should. Maybe if Adam saw that somebody else found her worth pursuing, he would get the same idea.

Tate had a cheerful smile on her face by the time she joined Adam in his office. He already had the computer on and was perusing the statistics she had input there.

"So what do you think?" she asked, perching herself on the arm of the large swivel chair in which he was sitting.

"It looks good." Of course his office wasn't as neat as it had once been. There were half-filled coffee cups amidst the clutter on the desk, and a collection of magazines and a dirty T-shirt decorated the floor. A bridle and several other pieces of tack Tate was fixing were strewn around the room.

But he couldn't argue with what she had accomplished. Tate had set up a program to handle data on each head of stock, providing a record that would be invaluable in making buying and selling decisions. "You didn't tell me you knew so much about computers."

Tate grinned and said, "You didn't ask." She leaned across him and began earnestly discussing other ideas she had regarding possible uses of the computer in his business.

He started automatically cleaning the debris from his desk.

"Don't worry about those," Tate said, taking a handful of pebbles from him. "Aren't they pretty? I found them down by the creek." She scattered them back onto the desk. "I play with them while I'm thinking, sort of like worry beads, you know?"

"Uh-huh."

Adam forced himself to concentrate on what she was saying, rather than the way her breast was pressed up against his arm. By the time she was done talking about the projects she had in mind, she had shifted position four times. He knew because she had managed to brush some part of his anatomy with some part of hers each time she moved.

Tate was totally oblivious to Adam's difficulty, because she was having her own problems concentrating on the matters at hand. She was busy planning how she could make Adam sit up and take notice of her by accepting Buck's invitation to go out tomorrow evening. She just had to make sure that Adam saw her leaving on the date with the auburn-haired cowboy.

Her thoughts must have conjured Buck, because he suddenly appeared at the door to Adam's office.

"Need you to take a look at that irrigation system to see whether you want it repaired or replaced," Buck said.

"I'll be right there," Adam replied.

Buck had already turned to leave when Tate realized she had

the perfect opportunity to let Adam know she was going out with another man. "Oh, Buck."

Buck turned and the hat came off his head in the same motion. "Yes, ma'am?"

"I've decided to take you up on your offer to go dancing tomorrow night."

Buck's face split with an engaging grin. "Yes, ma'am! I'll pick you up at seven o'clock if that's all right, and we can have some dinner first."

The thunderous look on Adam's face was everything Tate could have wished for. "I'll see you at seven," she promised.

Buck slipped his hat back on his head and said, "You coming, Boss?"

"In a minute. I'll catch up to you."

Adam's fists landed on his hips as he turned to confront Tate. "What was that all about?"

"Buck asked me to go dancing at Knippa on Saturday night, and I thought it might be fun."

Adam couldn't very well forbid her going. As Tate had so pointedly noted, he wasn't related to her in the least. But he couldn't help having misgivings, either. There was no telling what Buck Magnesson's reaction would be if Tate subjected him to the same teasing sensuality that Adam had endured for the past three weeks. If Tate said "Please" Buck was damned likely to say "Thank you" and take what she offered.

Adam suddenly heard himself forbidding his sister Melanie from going out on a date with a boy he had thought a little wild. Heard himself telling Melanie that he knew better than she what was best for her. And remembered the awful consequences of his high-handedness. Adam didn't have to like the fact that Tate had decided to go out with Buck Magnesson. But if he didn't want to repeat the mistakes he had made with his younger sister, he had to put up with it.

"Have a good time with Buck tomorrow night," he said. Then he turned and walked out the door.

Tate frowned at Adam's back. That wasn't exactly the reaction she had been hoping for. Where was the jealousy? Where was the demand that she spend her time with him instead? Suddenly Tate wished she had thought things through a little more carefully. Agreeing to date Buck simply to make Adam realize what he was missing wasn't turning out at all as she had hoped.

She felt a little guilty that she had even considered using Buck to make Adam jealous. But since her plan had failed—quite miserably—she could at least enjoy the evening with Buck with a clear conscience.

Tate had gotten the broken water hose fixed on her '51 Chevy, and she used the pickup to drive the ninety miles east to San Antonio that afternoon to go shopping. She could have worn jeans to go dancing, but had decided that she owed it to Buck to show up for their date looking her best.

She found a pretty halter sundress that tied around the neck and had an almost nonexistent back. The bodice fit her like a glove and showed just a hint of décolletage. The bright yellow and white floral print contrasted with her dark hair and picked up the gold in her eyes. The midcalf-length skirt was gathered at the waist and flared at the hem. She whirled once in front of the mirror and saw that the dress was going to reveal a great deal of her legs if Buck was the kind of dancer who liked to twirl his partner a lot.

Buck's smile when she opened the door on Saturday night

was well worth the effort spent shopping. She couldn't help feeling a stab of disappointment that Adam wasn't around to see her off. Apparently he had made plans of his own for the evening.

Tate found Buck surprisingly entertaining company. The cowboy had older brothers of his own, and Tate was quick to agree, "Nothing is harder to put up with than a good example!" He and Tate shared older brother horror stories that kept them both laughing through dinner.

The country and western band was in full swing when they crossed the threshold of the Grange Hall in Knippa. The room was fogged with cigarette smoke that battled with the overwhelming odor of sweat and cologne. The sawdusted dance floor was crowded, elbow to elbow, with men in cowboy hats partnered by ladies wearing flounced Western skirts and boots.

Just as they made their way to the dance floor, a two-step ended and the band began playing a waltz.

"Shall we?" Buck asked, making a dance frame with his arms.

"Absolutely!" Tate said, stepping into his embrace.

Tate got another welcome surprise when she and Buck began to waltz around the room. The lean cowboy was graceful on his feet. He led her into several intricate variations of the dance that left her breathless and feeling like a prima ballerina by the time the song ended.

"That was wonderful!" she exclaimed.

"Would you like something to drink?" Buck asked.

"Just a soda, please."

Buck found a seat for Tate at one of the small tables that surrounded the dance floor and forced his way through the crowd toward the bar.

Tate was tapping her foot to another two-step tune and enjoying watching the couples maneuver around the dance floor when she thought she saw someone she recognized. She followed the couple until they turned at the corner of the room.

Tate gasped aloud. It was Adam! He was dancing the two-step with a buxom redheaded woman.

As he passed by her table, Adam smiled and called out, "Hi, there! Having fun?"

Before she could answer, they had danced on past her, and she was left with the trill of the woman's laughter in her ears.

Tate felt sick. *Who was she?* The Redheaded Woman in Adam's arms was absolutely beautiful. No wonder Adam hadn't been interested in pursuing her when he was acquainted with such a gorgeous female.

"What's caught your eye?" Buck asked as he set a soda in front of Tate.

"Adam's here." She pointed him out. "See there. With that redhead."

To Tate's amazement, Buck scowled and swore under his breath.

"What's wrong?" she asked.

"Nothing I can do anything about."

"That's the sort of statement that's guaranteed to get a nosy female's attention," Tate said. "Out with it."

Buck grinned sheepishly and admitted, "All right. Here goes." He took a deep breath and said, "That woman dancing with Adam is my ex-wife."

"You're kidding!"

"'Fraid not."

Tate watched Buck watching the Redheaded Woman. His feelings were painfully transparent. "You're still in love with her."

Buck grimaced. "Much good it'll do me."

"I assume Adam knows how you feel."

"He asked my permission before he took Velma out the first time."

"And you gave it to him?" Tate asked incredulously.

"She isn't my wife anymore. She can see whoever she pleases."

Tate snorted in disgust. "While you suffer in noble silence. Men!"

Tate had been so involved with talking to Buck that she hadn't realized the song was ending. She was less than pleased when Adam and Velma arrived at their table.

"Mind if we join you?" Adam asked.

Tate bit her lip to keep from saying something censorable. She slipped her arm through Buck's, put a gigantic smile on her face, and said, "Why sure! We'd love to have the company, wouldn't we, Buck?"

It was hard to say who was the more surprised by her performance, Buck or Adam. What she hadn't expected was the militant light that rose in Velma's green eyes when Tate claimed Buck's arm. Well, well, well. Maybe there was more here than met the eye.

Adam made introductions, then seated Velma and caught one of the few waitresses long enough to ask for two drinks.

"I didn't expect to see you here," Tate said to Adam.

"I enjoy dancing, and Velma's a great partner."

Tate could imagine what else Velma was great at. She had observed for herself that the redhead had a wonderful sense of rhythm.

Tate was aware of Buck sitting stiffly beside her, quieter than he had been at any time during the evening. How could Adam not be sensitive to the vibrations that arced across the table between the cowboy and his ex-wife?

In fact, Adam was eminently aware of how much Buck Magnesson still loved his ex-wife. It was why he had brought Velma here this evening. Adam knew that with Velma in the room, Buck wasn't liable to spend much time thinking about Tate.

There was more than one way to skin a cat, Adam thought with satisfaction. He had known Tate would rebel against an ultimatum, so he hadn't protested her date with Buck. He had simply sought out a more subtle way to get what he wanted.

Bringing Velma to the dance seemed like the answer to his problem. He was pretty sure Velma was as much in love with Buck as the cowboy was with his ex-wife. He didn't mind playing Cupid, especially if it meant separating Tate from the virile young cowboy.

"How about trading partners?" Adam said, rising from his chair and reaching for Tate's hand.

Before Tate could protest, Buck said, "That sounds fine to me," took Velma by the hand and headed for the dance floor.

Tate wasn't sure what to make of Adam's ploy. She waited until they were half a dance floor away from the other couple before she said, "That was a pretty sneaky thing to do."

"I wanted to dance with you."

"Are you sure you aren't matchmaking?"

Adam smiled. "You could feel it, too?"

"I think he might still love her."

"I'm sure he does."

"Then why did you bring Velma here tonight?"

"I would think that's obvious."

"Not to me."

"I enjoy her company."

"Oh."

He grinned. "And I knew Buck would be here with you."

He sent her into a series of spins that prevented her from making any kind of retort. By the time she was in his arms again the song was over and he was ushering her back toward their table, where Buck and Velma were sitting across from each other arguing vociferously.

"Buck?" Tate didn't want to interrupt, but she wasn't sure whether she should leave him alone with Velma, either.

"Let's get out of here," Buck said, jumping up and turning his back on Velma. "Good night, Adam. I'll see you tomorrow."

As Buck hurried Tate away, she heard Velma say, "I'd like to go home now, Adam. If that's all right with you?"

Tate wasn't sure where Buck was taking her when he burned rubber on the asphalt parking lot. It was a safe guess from the dark look on his face that he had no romantic intentions toward her.

"Want to talk about it?" she asked at last.

Buck glanced quickly at her, then turned his eyes back to the road. "I don't want to bother you with my problems."

"I'm a good listener."

He sighed and said, "Velma and I were high school sweethearts. We married as soon as we graduated. Pretty soon Velma began to think she had missed something. She had an affair."

Tate bit her lip to keep from saying something judgmental. She was glad she had when Buck continued.

"I found out about it and confronted her. She asked for a divorce, and I gave it to her."

"Why?"

"Pride. Foolish damn pride!"

"And you regret it now?"

"My life's been running kind of muddy without her."

"So why don't you do something about it?" Tate asked.

"It's no use. She says that I deserve better. She doesn't believe I can ever forgive or forget what she did."

"Can you?"

The cowboy's eyes were bleak in the light from the dash. "I think so."

"But you're not sure?"

A muscle worked in his jaw. "If I were, I'd have her back home and under me faster than chain lightning with a link snapped!"

Tate had thought they were driving without direction, yet she realized suddenly that they had arrived back at the front door of Adam's house. She saw Adam's truck parked there. So, he was home. And there was a light on in the living room.

She let herself out of the truck, but Buck met her on the front porch. He put an arm around her waist and walked her away from the light.

"May I kiss you good-night, Tate?"

Tate drew a breath and held it. This was so exactly like the scene she had played out the night she had left home that it was eerie. Only there were no brothers here to protect her from the big, bad wolf.

"Of course you can kiss me good-night," she said at last.

Buck took his time, and Tate was aware of the sweetness of

his kiss. And the reluctance in it. When he lifted his head their eyes met, and they smiled at each other.

"No go, huh?" he said.

Tate shook her head. "I like you an awful lot, Buck. I hope we can be friends."

"I'd like that," the cowboy said.

He leaned down and kissed her again. Both of them knew how much—and how little—it meant.

However, it was not so clear to the man watching them through a slit in the living room curtains.

Chapter 5

IT HAD TAKEN EVERY OUNCE of willpower Adam possessed to keep from stalking out onto the front porch and putting his fist in Buck Magnesson's nose. It wasn't just the thought of his sister Melanie that kept him from doing it. There were things he couldn't offer Tate that Buck could.

But he wasn't a saint or a eunuch. If Tate persisted in tempting him, he wasn't noble enough to refuse her. He was determined to keep his hunger leashed at least until he was certain Tate knew what she *wouldn't* be getting if she got involved with him. She was too young to give up her dreams. And there was no way he could fulfill them.

Before Adam had time to examine his feelings further, the front door opened. Tate stepped inside to find him sitting in one of the large Mediterranean chairs before the blackened fireplace, nursing a half-empty glass of whiskey.

"Hello," she said. "I didn't expect to see you again tonight."

"I was waiting up for you."

Tate immediately bristled. "Look, I don't need a caretaker."

She wanted a lover. But not just that. A man who loved her, as she was beginning to fear she loved him.

"Old habits die hard."

"What's that supposed to mean?"

"I used to wait up for my sister Melanie."

"You have a sister? Why haven't I met her?"

"She died ten years ago."

"I'm so sorry."

Adam had drunk just enough whiskey to want to tell her the rest of it. "Melanie ran away from home when she was seventeen. She was picked up by a stranger while hitchhiking. He raped her, and then he stabbed her to death."

"That must have been awful for you!" Tate wanted to put her arms around Adam to comfort him, but his body language posted obvious No Trespassing signs.

She used sitting on the couch as an excuse to cross closer to him, slipped off her boots and pulled her feet up under her. She folded her arms under her breasts to give herself the comfort he wouldn't accept.

Then another, more troubling thought occurred to her. "Is that why you picked me up on the road? Because of your sister?"

Adam nodded.

Tate felt as though she'd been physically struck. She hesitated and asked, "Is that why you offered me a job?"

"It seemed like a good idea at the time."

Tate swallowed over the lump that had grown in her throat. "So I'm just a charity case to you?"

Adam heard the pain in Tate's voice and realized he had handled this all wrong. If he didn't do some fast talking, he knew she would be gone by morning. "You can hardly blame me for offering help under the circumstances, can you? I couldn't take the chance that I might be responsible for another young woman's death!"

Tate wasn't so wrapped up in her own feelings that she failed to recognize the significance of what Adam had just said. "How can you blame yourself for your sister's death? What happened couldn't possibly be your fault!"

"Oh, no?" Adam's nostrils were pinched, his blue eyes like shards of ice. "Didn't you tell me that you left home because your brothers made your life miserable?"

"They only did what they did because they love me!" Tate protested.

"So that makes it all right for them to interfere in your life? To aggravate you enough to send you running in that old rattletrap truck?"

It was clear Adam was searching for answers that would release him from the guilt he suffered over what had happened to his sister. Tate found herself equally confounded by the issues he had raised. Was love a good enough excuse for the high-handed way Garth and Faron had acted? What if she had met the same fate as Adam's sister? Would they have blamed themselves for her death?

She knew they would have, just as Adam had blamed himself for Melanie's death all these years. She didn't know what to say to ease his pain. She only knew she had to do something.

Tate stood and crossed to Adam. She knelt on the cool tile floor at his feet and laid a hand on his thigh. She felt him tense beneath her touch. "Adam, I—"

He rose abruptly and stalked away from her. "I'm not in the mood for any teasing tonight."

"I was trying to offer comfort!" Tate retorted.

"Just stay away from me!"

Tate struck back like the scorned woman she felt herself to be. "There are plenty of others who'll welcome my attentions!"

"Like Buck?"

"Like Buck!" That was a lie, but told in a good cause. Saving her pride seemed of utmost importance right now.

"He'll never marry you. He's still in love with Velma."

Since Tate knew he was right, she retorted, "I don't have to marry a man to go to bed with him!"

"Is that so, *little girl?*"

Tate was gasping, she was so furious at the taunting words. But it was clear she could cut her own throat with a sharp tongue. She had certainly dug a hole for herself it was going to be hard to get out of. She took two deep breaths, trying to regain her temper.

Adam didn't give her a chance to speak before he said, "If you're smart, you'll go back home where you belong. Now, before you get hurt."

"Are you firing me?"

Tate held her breath until he said, "No."

"Then I'm staying. If you'll excuse me, I'm tired. I want to go to bed."

Tate had started for the door when Adam quipped, "What, no invitation to join you?"

Tate slowly turned back to face him. She took her time getting from where she was to where he was. She hooked a finger into the opening at the neck of his shirt and looked up into eyes that were both wary and amused.

"I learned at my brothers' knees never to approach a bull

from the front, a horse from the rear…or a damn fool from any direction. Good night, Adam."

"We'll talk about this again tomorrow," he said to her retreating back.

"Like hell we will!" she replied.

Tate spent a restless night, tossing and turning as her mind grappled with all of Adam's revelations. What she found most disturbing was the possibility that Adam had merely been tolerating her because he felt responsible for her welfare.

Surely she couldn't have been mistaken about his physical reaction to her! More likely, he was attracted to her, but his feelings of responsibility toward her were keeping him from pursuing a relationship. If so, she would soon cure him of that!

Tate felt somewhat cheered by her decision, and she made up her mind to confront Adam at breakfast. Only, when she arrived in the kitchen the next morning, she discovered that he had already eaten and left the house.

"Did he say where he was going, Maria?"

"No, *señorita*."

Tate worked hard all day in the office so she wouldn't have time to worry about where Adam had gone. He was bound to turn up sooner or later. He wasn't going anywhere. And neither was she.

However, by seven o'clock that evening there was still no sign of Adam. He hadn't even called Maria to say he wouldn't be home for dinner. Maria was washing up the dinner dishes, and to keep herself busy, Tate was drying them and putting them away. Maria had tried to start a conversation, but Tate was too distracted to keep track of what she was saying. Finally Maria gave up trying and left Tate to her thoughts.

Tate was worried. Where could Adam have gone? She had already checked once at the bunkhouse, but no one had seen him all day.

When she heard a knock at the kitchen door, Tate leaped to answer it. It wasn't until she opened the door that she realized Adam wouldn't have knocked.

"Buck! You look terrible. What's wrong?"

Buck pulled his hat off his head and wiped the sweat from his brow with his sleeve. "Um, I, um."

She put a hand on his arm and urged him inside the room. "Come in. Sit down."

He resisted her efforts to move him from his spot just inside the kitchen door. "No, I—"

"You what?" Tate asked in exasperation.

"I need your help."

"Of course, anything."

"Maybe you better not say yes until you hear what I have to say." He eyed Maria, but was too polite to ask her to leave.

Aware of the tension in the cowboy, Maria said, "I give you some time alone, so you can talk," and left the room. But she made up her mind she wouldn't be gone for long. The nice *señorita,* she was good for Señor Adam. It would not do to let cowboys like Buck Magnesson take what should not be theirs.

Tate turned a kitchen chair and sat in it like a saddle. "I'm all ears."

Buck fidgeted with the brim of his hat another moment before he said, "I've thought a lot about our conversation last night. You know, about whether or not I could forgive and forget what Velma did? And, well…I believe I can."

A smile spread on Tate's face. "I'm so glad, Buck."

"Yeah, well, that's why I need your help. I've decided to go see Velma and tell her how I feel, and I thought maybe if you were along to sort of referee—"

Tate was up and across the room in an instant. She gave the startled cowboy a big hug. "It'll be my pleasure. When would you like to go see her?"

Buck grinned. "Is right now too soon?"

Tate thought about leaving a note for Adam, then rejected the idea. It would do him good to know how it felt to worry about someone who didn't leave a message where he was going!

Maria heard the kitchen door slam closed and came back in to see what Señor Buck had wanted. She frowned and clucked her tongue in dismay when she realized that Señorita Tate had left the house with the handsome cowboy. "Señor Adam will not like this. He will not like this at all."

Maria made up her mind to stay until Señor Adam got back from wherever he had gone and tell him what had happened. Then he could go find the *señorita* and bring her home where she belonged.

Meanwhile, Buck drove Tate to a tiny house with gingerbread trim in a quiet neighborhood off Main Street in Uvalde. She waited anxiously with him to see if Velma was going to answer the doorbell.

Tate saw the light in Velma's green eyes when she saw Buck, and watched it die when she realized Tate was with him.

"I want to talk to you, Velma," Buck said.

"I don't think we have anything to say to each other." She nearly had the door closed when Buck stuck his boot in it.

"I'm not leaving until I say my piece," Buck insisted in a harsh voice.

"I'll call the police if you don't go away," Velma threatened.

"I just want to talk!"

When Velma let go of the door to run for the phone, Buck and Tate took advantage of the opportunity to come inside. Buck caught Velma in the kitchen and pried the phone receiver out of her hand.

"Please, baby, just listen to me," he pleaded.

"Please give him a chance, Velma. I know you're going to want to hear what Buck has to say."

Velma froze when she heard Tate's voice. "Why did you come here?" she demanded.

"Buck thought it might make it easier for the two of you to talk if there was someone else here to sort of mediate."

Velma looked at Buck's somber face. She took a deep breath and said, "All right. I'll listen to what you have to say. For five minutes."

Buck set her down, letting her body slide along his as he did. Tate could have lit a fire from the sparks that flew between them. They belonged together, all right. She only hoped Buck would find the right words to convince Velma he meant what he said.

Five minutes later, Velma was still listening, but Tate could see she was torn between the fervent wish to believe Buck, and the awful fear that he would soon regret what he was saying.

"I don't think I'll ever forget what happened, Velma," Buck said. "But I think I can live with it."

That wasn't exactly the same thing as *forgiving* it, Tate realized. Apparently Velma also noticed the distinction.

"That's not good enough, Buck," she said in a quiet voice.

"I love you, Velma," he said.

She choked on a sob. "I know, Buck. I love you, too."

"Then why can't we get back together?"

"It just wouldn't work."

By now Velma was crying in earnest, and Buck would have been heartless indeed if he could have resisted pulling her into his arms to comfort her. In fact, that was just what he did.

Tate suddenly realized another reason why she had been brought along. Her presence provided the only restraint on the sexual explosion that occurred whenever the two of them touched. Even that wasn't sufficient at first.

Buck already had his fingers twined in Velma's red curls, and Velma had her hand on the front of Buck's jeans when Tate cleared her throat loudly to remind them that she was still there. They broke apart like two teenagers caught necking, their faces flushed as much by embarrassment as by passion.

"Uh, sorry," Buck said.

Velma tried rearranging her hair, a hopeless task considering how badly Buck had messed it up.

"You look fine, honey," Buck said, taking a hand at smoothing her tresses himself. But the gesture turned into a caress, which turned into a fervent look of desire, which ended when Buck's lips lowered to Velma's in the gentlest of kisses.

There was no telling where things might have gone from there, except Tate said, "All right, enough is enough! We'll never get anywhere this way. Buck, you go sit over there in that chair. Velma and I will sit on the couch."

Sheepishly, Buck crossed the room and slouched down in the chair Tate had indicated. Tate joined Velma on the couch. She dragged her T-shirt out of her jeans and used it to dab at Velma's tears.

"Now it seems to me," Tate began, "that you both want to give this relationship another try. So I have a suggestion."

Tate outlined for them a plan whereby they would start from scratch. Buck would pick Velma up at her door, they would go out together and he would return her at the end of the evening. Absolutely no sex.

"You have to learn to trust each other again," she said. "That takes time."

Buck's face had taken on a mulish cast. "I'm not sure I can play by those rules. Especially that 'no sex' part."

It wasn't hard to see why. The sexual electricity between them would have killed a normal person.

"No sex," Tate insisted. "If you spend all your time in bed, you won't do as much talking. And you both have a lot you need to talk about."

Tate chewed anxiously on her lower lip while she waited to see whether they would accept her suggestion.

"I think Tate's right," Velma said.

The negotiations didn't end there. In fact it wasn't until the wee hours of the morning that all parties were satisfied. Tate felt as emotionally exhausted as she knew Buck and Velma were. The hug Velma gave her as she was leaving, and the whispered "Thank you" from the other woman, made everything worthwhile.

Tate rubbed the tense muscles in her neck as Buck drove her back to the ranch. She knew Buck was still troubled, but at least now there was some hope that he and his ex-wife might one day end up together again.

When they arrived at the front door to Adam's house, Buck took Tate's hand in his and said, "I don't know how to thank you."

"Just be good to Velma. That'll be thanks enough for me."

He ruffled her hair as an older brother might, then leaned over and kissed her on the cheek. "You're a good friend, Tate. If I can ever do anything for you, just let me know."

"I'll remember that," Tate said. "You don't need to get out. I can let myself in."

Buck waited until she was inside the front door before he drove his truck around to the bunkhouse.

Tate had only taken two steps when the living room lights clicked on. Adam stood at the switch, his face a granite mask of displeasure.

"Where were you?" Tate accused. "I waited for you for hours, but you never came home!"

Adam was taken aback, since he had intended to ask the same question. "Dr. Kowalski had a medical emergency with one of my former patients. Susan asked me to come because Mrs. Daniels was frightened, and she thought the old lady would respond better if I was there."

"I knew it had to be something important," Tate said with a sigh of relief. "Were you able to help?"

"Yes, Mrs. Daniels is out of danger now."

Adam suddenly realized that Tate had completely distracted him from the confrontation he had planned. His eyes narrowed as he tried to decide whether she had done it on purpose.

"Where have you been all night?" he asked in a cool voice. "Do you realize it's four a.m.?"

"Is it really that late? I mean, that early," Tate said with a laugh. "I was out with Buck. Oh, Adam—"

He cut her off with a snarl of disgust as she confirmed his worst suspicions. "I don't suppose I have to ask what you were doing, *little girl*. If you were that anxious to lose your virginity you should have told me. You didn't have to drag Buck into the picture."

Tate was aghast. "You think Buck and I—"

"What am I supposed to think when you come rolling in at this ungodly hour of the morning with your T-shirt hanging out and your hair mussed up and your lower lip swollen like it's been bitten a dozen times."

"There's a perfectly logical—"

"I don't want to hear any excuses! Do you deny that you spent the night with Buck?"

"No, but something wonderful happened—"

"I don't want to hear the gory details!"

He was shouting by now, and Tate knew that if she had been any closer Adam might not have been able to control the visible anger that shook his body.

"Get out of my sight!" he said in hard, quiet voice. "Before I do something I'll regret."

Tate put her chin up. If this *fool* would give her a chance, she could explain everything! But her pride goaded her to remain silent. Adam was neither father nor brother. Yet he seemed determined to fill the role of protector. She felt the tears that threatened. Why couldn't he see that she only had eyes for one man—and that man was him!

"Some folks can't see any farther than the steam from their own pot of stew." With that pronouncement, she turned and stalked from the room.

Once Tate was gone, Adam swore a blue streak. When he was done, he felt worse instead of better. He had hoped he was wrong about what Tate and Buck had been doing out so late. He had been stunned when Tate hadn't denied losing her virginity to the cowboy. He felt absolute, uncontrollable rage at the thought of some other man touching her in ways he knew she had never been touched. And the thought that she had found it *wonderful* caused an unbearable tightness in his chest.

He tried to tell himself that what had happened was for the best. He was not a whole man. She deserved more. But nothing he said to himself took away the bitter taste in his mouth. She was his. She belonged to him.

And by God, now that her virginity was no longer an impediment, he would have her.

Chapter 6

SUDDENLY IT WAS ADAM who became the pursuer and Tate who proved elusive. She gave him the cold shoulder whenever she met him and made a point of smiling and recklessly flirting with Buck. Because of the way Buck's courtship was prospering with Velma, he had the look of a happy, well-satisfied man. Which left Adam seething with jealousy.

Tate suspected she could lift the thundercloud that followed Adam around if she simply told him the truth about what she had been doing the night she had spent with Buck. But she was determined that Adam would be the one to make the first move toward conciliation. All he had done for the past week was glare daggers at her.

However, there was more than anger reflected in his gaze, more than antagonism in his attitude toward her. Tate was beginning to feel frazzled by the unspoken sexual tension that sizzled between them. Something had changed since the night they had argued, and Tate felt the hairs lift on her arms whenever Adam was around. His look was hungry. His body radiated leashed power. His features were harsh with unsatisfied need. She had the uneasy feeling he was stalking her.

Tate escaped into the office by day, and played mediator for Buck and Velma at night. She refused to admit that she was hiding from Adam, but that was the case. His eyes followed her whenever they were in the same room together, and she knew he must be aware of her reaction to his disconcerting gaze.

Exactly one week from the day Tate had accompanied Buck on his pivotal visit to Velma, the cowboy took Tate aside and asked whether she minded staying home that evening instead of joining them as chaperon.

"There are some things I'd like to discuss with Velma alone," Buck said.

"Why sure," Tate replied with a forced smile. "I don't mind at all."

Once Buck was gone, Tate's smile flattened into a somber line. She was more than a little worried about what Adam might do if he found out she was home for the evening. She decided the best plan was to avoid him by staying in her room. It was the coward's way out, but her brothers had taught her that sometimes it was best to play your cards close to your belly.

Tate quickly found herself bored within the confines of her bedroom. She remembered that there was some work she could do in the office—if only she could get there without being detected by Adam. The light was on in his bedroom across the courtyard. Adam often retired early and did his reading—both ranch and medical journals—in bed.

She was already dressed for sleep in a long pink T-shirt, but it covered her practically to the knees. She decided it was modest enough even for Adam should he find her working late in the office. She tiptoed barefoot across the tiled court-yard, which was lit by both moon and stars, slipped into Adam's wing of the house via a door at the far end, and sneaked down the hall to the office.

It could have been an hour later, or two, when Tate sud-denly felt the hairs prickle on her arms. She had long since fin-ished working at the computer. Because the chair in front of the desk was more comfortable than the one behind it—which was as straight-backed and rigid as the man who usually sat there—she had plopped down in it to look over the printout of what she had done. She had one ankle balanced on the front of the desk and the other hooked on the opposite knee.

She glanced up and found herself ensnared by the look of desire in Adam's heavy-lidded blue eyes.

"Working late?" he asked in a silky voice.

"I thought I'd finish a few things."

Tate was frozen, unable to move, uncomfortably aware that her long T-shirt had rucked up around her thighs, and that her legs were bare all the way up to yonder. As Adam stared in-tently at her, she felt her nipples harden into dark buds easily visible beneath the pink cotton.

Adam's chest was bare, revealing dark curls that arrowed down into his Levi's. His jeans seemed to be hanging on his hipbones. His belly was ribbed with muscle, and a faint sheen of perspiration made his skin glow in the light from the sin-gle standing lamp.

Adam was no less disconcerted by Tate's appearance. He had come to his office looking for a ranch journal and found a sul-try sex kitten instead. His view of Tate's French-cut panties was wreaking havoc with his self-control. Her crow-black hair was tousled, and her whiskey-colored eyes were dark with feminine allure.

"You ought to know better than to come here half-dressed," Adam said.

"I wasn't expecting to see you."

One black brow arched disbelievingly. "Weren't you?"

Adam abruptly swept the desk clear of debris with one hand while he reached for Tate with the other. Papers flew in the air, cups shattered, Tate's handful of pebbles pinged as they shot across the tile floor. The last paper hadn't landed, nor the pinging sound faded, when he set her down hard on the edge of the desk facing him.

Tate's frightened protest died on her lips. Adam's fierce blue eyes never left hers as he spread her legs and stepped between them. He yanked her toward him, fitting the thin silk of her panties snugly against the heat and hardness of his arousal.

"Is this what you had in mind?" he demanded.

"Adam, I—"

She gasped as rough hands smoothed the cotton over her breasts, revealing nipples that ached for his touch.

"Adam—"

"You've been teasing me for weeks, *little girl*. Even I have my limits. You're finally going to get what you've been asking for."

"Adam—"

"Shut up, Tate."

He seized both her hands in one of his and thrust his fingers into the hair at her nape to hold her captive for his kiss.

Tate didn't dare breathe as Adam lowered his head to hers. Her body was alive with anticipation. Though she had wanted this ever since she had first laid eyes on Adam, she was still a little afraid of what was to come. She wanted this man, and she was certain now that he wanted her. Tonight she would know what it meant to be a woman, to be Adam's woman. The waiting was over at last.

Adam's anger at finding what he considered a sensual trap in his office made him more forceful with Tate than he had intended. But after all, she was no longer the tender, inexperienced virgin of a week ago.

However, somewhere between the moment he laced his hand into her hair and the instant his lips reached hers, his feelings underwent a violent transformation. Powerful emotions were at work, soothing the savage beast. When they finally kissed, there was nothing in his touch beyond the fierce need for her that thrummed through his body.

Tate was unprepared for the velvety softness of Adam's lips as he slid his mouth across hers. His teeth found her lower lip, and she shivered as he nipped it and then soothed the hurt. His tongue teased her, slipping inside, then retreating until she sought it out and discovered the taste of him. Dark and distinctive and uniquely male.

Tate was lost in sensation as each kiss was answered by a streak of desire that found its way to her belly. Her breasts felt full and achy, yet she was too inexperienced to ask for the touch that would have satisfied her body's yearning.

Sometime while she was being kissed, Adam had released her hands. Tate wasn't quite sure what to do with them. She sought out his shoulders, then slid her hands down his back, feeling the corded muscle and sinew that made him so different from her.

Her head fell back as Adam's mouth caressed the hollow in her throat. The male hands at her waist slowly slid up under her T-shirt until Adam was cupping her breasts. Tate gasped as his thumbs brushed across the aching crests. Her body seemed alive to the barest touch of his callused fingertips.

"I want to feel you against me," Adam said as he slipped the pink T-shirt off over her head.

Before Tate could feel embarrassed, his arms slid around her.

He sighed with satisfaction as he hugged her to him. "You feel so good," he murmured against her throat.

Tate's breasts were excruciatingly sensitive to the wiry texture of Adam's chest hair. She was intimately aware of his strength, of her own softness.

Adam grasped her thighs and pulled her more snugly against him. She clutched his shoulders and held on as his maleness pressed against her femininity, evoking feelings that were foreign, yet which coaxed an instinctive response.

A guttural groan escaped Adam as Tate arched her body into his. His hands dug into her buttocks, trying to hold her still.

"You're killing me, sweetheart," he said. "Don't move!"

"But it feels good," Tate protested.

Adam half groaned, half laughed. "Too good," he agreed. "Be still. I want to be sure you enjoy this as much as I do."

"Oh, I will," Tate assured him.

Adam chuckled as he slid his mouth down her throat. He captured a nipple in his mouth, sucked on it, teased it with his tongue, then sucked again, until Tate was writhing with pleasure in his arms.

He took one of her hands and slid it along the hard ridge in his jeans, too wrapped up in the pleasure of the moment to notice her virginal reluctance to touch him. "Feel what you do to me," he said. "I only have to look at you, think about you, and I want you!" His chin rested at her temple, and he was aware of the faint scent of lilacs. He would always think of her from now on when he smelled that particular fragrance.

It didn't take Tate long to realize how sensitive Adam was to her barest touch, and she reveled in her newfound feminine power.

When he could stand the pleasure no longer, Adam brought each of Tate's hands to his mouth, kissed her wrists and her palms, then placed her hands flat on his chest. "Lift your hips, sweetheart," Adam murmured as he tucked his thumbs into her bikini panties.

She did as he asked, and an instant later Tate was naked. She hid her face in his shoulder, suddenly shy with him.

Adam's arms slipped around her. "There's no need to be embarrassed, sweetheart," he teased.

"That's easy to say when you've got clothes on," she retorted.

Adam laughed. "That can be easily remedied."

He reached between them and unsnapped his jeans. The harsh rasp of the zipper filled a silence broken only by the sound of her labored breathing, and his.

Tate grabbed Adam's wrist to keep him from pulling his zipper down any more. "Not yet," she said breathlessly.

She couldn't help the nerves that assailed her. Adam seemed to think she knew what to do, and perhaps she had led him to believe it was so, but she was all too aware of her ignorance—and innocence.

He dragged the zipper back up but left the snap undone. "There's no hurry, sweetheart. We have all night."

Tate shivered—as much from a virgin's qualms as from anticipation—at the thought.

Adam settled her hands at his waist and lifted his own to gently cup her face. He angled her chin so that she was looking up at him. "You're so damn beautiful!" he said.

"Your eyes." He kissed them closed.

"Your nose." He cherished the tip of it.

"Your cheeks." He gave each one an accolade.

"Your chin." He nipped it with his teeth.

"Your mouth."

Tate's eyes had slipped closed as Adam began his reverent seduction. She waited with bated breath for the kiss that didn't come. Suddenly she felt herself being lifted into his arms. Her eyes flashed open in alarm.

"Adam! What are you doing? Where are we going?"

He was already halfway down the hall to his room when he said, "I want the pleasure of making love to you for the first time in my own bed."

Tate had peeked into Adam's bedroom, but she had never been invited inside. It was decorated in warm earth tones, sandy browns and cinnamon. She had remembered being awed by the sheer size of his bed. The antique headboard was an intricately carved masterpiece, and the spindles at head and foot nearly reached to the ten-foot ceiling.

The quilt that covered the bed was an intricate box design Tate had never seen before, but the craftsmanship was exquisite. Tate grabbed Adam around the neck to keep from falling when he reached down to yank the quilt aside, revealing pristine white sheets.

"Now we can relax and enjoy ourselves," he said.

Adam laid her on the bed and in the same motion used his body to mantle hers. He nudged her legs apart with his knees and settled himself against her so that she was left in no doubt as to the reason he had brought her here.

"Where did you get this bed?" Tate asked, postponing the moment of ultimate truth.

"It's a family heirloom. Several generations of my ancestors have been conceived and born here."

But not my own, Adam thought. *Never my own.*

Tate felt the sudden tension in his body. "Adam?"

Adam's features hardened as he recalled what had happened over the past week to cause him to be here now with Tate. She had made her choice. And he had made his. He wanted her, and she was willing. That was all that mattered now.

Adam's kiss was fierce, and Tate was caught up in the roughness of his lovemaking. There was nothing brutal about his caresses, but they were not gentle, either. His kisses were fervent, his passion unbridled, as he drove her ruthlessly toward a goal she could only imagine.

Tate was hardly aware when Adam freed himself of his clothes. She was so lost in new sensations that the feel of his hard naked body against hers was but one of many delights. The feel of his hands…*there.* The feel of his lips and tongue…*there.*

Tate was in ecstasy bordering on pain. She reached with trembling hands for whatever part of Adam she could find with her hands and her mouth.

"Adam, please!" She didn't know what she wanted, only that she desperately needed…*something.* Her body arched toward his, wild with need.

Just as Adam lifted her hips for his thrust, she cried, "Wait!" But it was already too late.

Adam's face paled as he realized what he had done.

Tate's fingernails bit into his shoulder, and she clamped her teeth on her lower lip to keep from crying out. Tears of pain pooled in the corners of her eyes.

Adam felt her muscles clench involuntarily around him and struggled not to move, fearing he would hurt her more. "You didn't sleep with Buck," he said in a flat voice.

"No," she whispered.

"You were still a virgin."

"Yes," she whispered.

"Why did you make me think— Dammit to hell, Tate! I would have done things differently if I'd known. I wouldn't have—"

He started to pull out of her, but she clutched at his shoulders. "Please, Adam. It's done now. Make love to me."

Tate lifted her hips, causing Adam to grunt with pleasure.

Now that he knew how inexperienced she was, Adam tried to be gentle. But Tate took matters out of his hands, touching him in places that sent his pulse through the roof, taunting him with her mouth and hands, until his thrust was almost savage. He brought them both to a climax so powerful that it left them gasping.

Adam slid to Tate's side and folded her in his embrace. He reached down to pull the covers over them and saw the blood on the sheet that testified to her innocence.

It made him angry all over again.

"I hope you're pleased with yourself!"

"Yes, I am."

"Don't expect an offer of marriage, because you're not going to get it," he said bluntly.

Tate fumbled for a sheet to cover herself. She sat up and

stared at Adam with wary eyes. "I don't think I expected any such thing."

"No? What about all those dreams of yours—meeting the right man, having a nice home and a gaggle of children playing at your feet?"

"Geese come in a gaggle," she corrected. "And for your information, I don't think my dream is the least bit unreasonable."

"It is if you have me pictured in the role of Prince Charming."

Tate flushed. She toyed with the sheet, arranging it to cover her naked flank.

Adam watched with regret as her tempting flesh disappeared from view. "Well, Tate?"

She looked into eyes still darkened with passion and said with all the tenderness she felt for him, "I love you, Adam."

"That was lust, not love."

Tate winced at the vehemence with which he denied the rightness of what had just happened between them.

"Besides," he added, "I like my women a little more experienced."

Adam did nothing to temper the pain he saw in Tate's face at his brutal rejection of her. He couldn't give her what she wanted, and he refused to risk the pain and humiliation of having her reject what little he could offer.

"If what you want is sex, I'm available," he said. "But I'm not in love with you, Tate. And I won't pretend I am."

Tate fought the tears that threatened. She would be *damned* if she would let him see how devastated she was by his refusal to acknowledge the beautiful experience they had shared.

"It wasn't just sex, Adam," she said. "You're only fooling yourself if you think it was."

His lips curled sardonically. "When you've had a little more experience you'll realize that any man can do the same thing for you."

"Even Buck?" she taunted.

A muscle jumped in Adam's jaw. She knew all the right buttons to push where he was concerned. "You get the hankering for a little sex, you come see *me*," he drawled. "*I'll* make sure you're satisfied, *little girl*."

Tate pulled the sheet free of the mattress and wrapped it around herself as best she could. "Good night, Adam. I think I'll sleep better in my own bed."

He watched her go without saying another word. The instant she was gone he pounded a fist into the mattress.

"Damn you, Tate Whitelaw!"

She had made him wish for something he could never have. She had offered him the moon and the stars. All he had to do was bare his soul to her. And take the heart-wrenching chance that she would reject what little he could offer in return.

Chapter 7

THE TEARS TATE HAD refused to let Adam see her shed fell with a vengeance once she was alone. But she hadn't been raised to give up or give in. Before long Tate had brushed the tears aside and begun to plan how best to make Adam eat his words.

If Adam hadn't cared for her at least a little, Tate reasoned, he wouldn't have been so upset by her taunt that she would seek out Buck. She was certain that Adam's jealousy could be a powerful weapon in her battle to convince him that they belonged together. Especially since Adam had admitted that he was willing to take extreme measures—even making love to her!—to keep her away from Buck. Tate intended to seek Buck out and let the green-eyed monster eat Adam alive.

It was with some distress and consternation that Tate realized over the next several days that Adam had somehow turned the tables on her. He was the one who found excuses to send her off alone with Buck. And he did it with a smile on his face.

Where was the green-eyed monster? Was it possible Adam really *didn't* care? He was obviously pushing her in Buck's direction. Was this some sort of test? Did he expect her to fall into Buck's arms? Did he *want* her to?

If Tate was unsure of Adam's intentions, he was no less confused himself. He had woken up the morning after making love to Tate and realized that somewhere between the moment she had first flashed that gamine smile at him and the moment he had claimed her with his body, he had fallen in love with her. It was an appalling realization, coming, as it had, after he had insulted and rejected her.

Loving Tate meant being willing to do what was best for her—even if it meant giving her up. He had made the selflessly noble—if absurd—decision that if, after the way he had treated her, she would rather be with Buck, he would not stand in her way. So he had made excuses for them to be alone together. And suffered the agonies of the damned, wondering whether Buck was taking advantage of the time to make love to her.

One or the other of them might have relented and honestly admitted their feelings, but they weren't given the chance before circumstances caused the tension-fraught situation to explode.

Adam had gritted his teeth and nobly sent Tate off with Buck to the Saturday night dance at the Grange Hall in Knippa, not realizing that they were stopping to pick up Velma on the way.

Tate didn't lack for partners at the dance, but she was on her way to a wretchedly lonely evening nonetheless—because the one person she wanted to be with wasn't there. She refused a cowboy the next dance so she could catch her breath. Unfortunately, that gave her time to think.

She found herself admitting that she might as well give up on her plan to make Adam jealous, mainly because it wasn't working. If he truly didn't want her, she would have to leave the Lazy S. Because she couldn't stand to be around him knowing that the love she felt would never be returned.

An altercation on the dance floor dragged Tate from her morose reflections. She was on her feet an instant later when she realized that one of the two men slugging away at each other was Buck Magnesson.

She reached Velma's side and shouted over the ruckus, "What happened? Why are they fighting?"

"All the poor man did was wink at me!" Velma shouted back. "It didn't mean a thing! There was no reason for Buck to take a swing at him."

When Tate looked back to the fight it was all over. The cowboy who had winked at Velma was out cold, and Buck was blowing cool air on his bruised knuckles. He was sporting a black eye and a cut on his chin, but his smile was broad and satisfied.

"Guess he won't be making any more advances to you, honey," Buck said.

"You idiot! You animal! I don't know when I've ever been so humiliated in my entire life!" Velma raged.

"But, honey—"

"How could you?"

"But, honey—"

Tate and Buck were left standing as Velma turned in a huff and headed for the door. Buck threw some money on the table to pay for their drinks and raced outside after her.

Velma was draped across the hood of the pickup, her face hidden in her crossed arms as she sobbed her heart out.

When Buck tried to touch her, she whirled on him. "Stay away from me!"

"What did I do?" he demanded, getting angry now.

"You don't even know, do you?" she sobbed.

"No, I don't, so I'd appreciate it if you'd just spit it out."

"You didn't trust me!" she cried.

"What?"

"You didn't trust me to let that cowboy know I'm not in-terested. You took it upon yourself to make sure he'd keep his distance.

"You're never going to forget the fact that I strayed once, Buck. You're always going to be watching—waiting to see if I slip up again. And every time you do something to remind me that you don't trust me—like you did tonight—it'll hurt the way it hurts right now.

"I won't be able to stand it, Buck. It'll kill me to love you and know you're watching me every minute from the corner of your eye. Take me home. I never want to see you again!"

Velma sat on the outside edge of the front seat, with Tate in the middle during the long, silent fifteen-minute drive west to Uvalde from Knippa. When they arrived in Velma's drive-way, she jumped out and went running into the house before Buck could follow her.

Buck crossed his arms on the steering wheel and dropped his forehead onto them. "God. I feel awful."

Tate didn't know what to say. So she just waited for him to talk.

"I couldn't help myself," he said. "When I saw that fellow looking at her…I don't know, I just went crazy."

"Because you were afraid he would make a move on Velma?"

"Yeah."

"Is Velma right, Buck? Didn't you trust her to say no on her own?"

Buck sighed. It was a defeated sound. "No."

There wasn't anything else to say. Buck had thought he could forgive and forget. But when it came right down to it, he would never trust Velma again. The risk was too great that his trust would prove unfounded.

"I don't want to be alone right now," Buck said. "Would you mind driving up toward the Frio with me? Maybe we can find a comfortable place to sit along the riverbank and lie back and count the stars. Just for a while," he promised. "I won't keep you out too late."

Tate knew Adam might be waiting up for her, but Buck had promised he wouldn't keep her out late. Besides, Adam's behavior over the past few days—throwing her into Buck's company—suggested that he no longer cared one way or the other.

"All right, Buck. Let's go. I could use some time away to think myself."

They found a spot beneath some immense cypress trees, and lay back on the grassy bank and listened to the wind whistling through the boughs. They tried to find the constellations and the North Star in the cloudless blue-black sky. The burble of the water over the rocky streambed was soothing to two wounded souls.

They talked about nothing, and everything. About childhood hopes and dreams. And adult realities. About wishes that never came true. They talked until their eyes drifted closed.

And they fell asleep.

Tate woke first. A mosquito was buzzing in her ear. She slapped at it, and when it came back again she sat up abruptly. And realized where she was. And who was lying beside her. And what time it was.

She shook Buck hard and said, "Wake up! It's dawn already. We must have fallen asleep. We've got to get home!"

Buck was used to rising early, but a night on the cold hard ground—not to mention the events of the previous evening— had left him grumpy. "I'm going, I'm going," he muttered as Tate shoved him toward the truck.

Tate sat on the edge of her seat the whole way home. She only hoped she could sneak into the house before Adam saw her. She could imagine what he would think if he saw her with grass stains on her denim skirt and a blouse that looked as if she had slept in it—which she had. Adam would never believe it had been a totally innocent evening.

When Buck dropped her off, she ran up the steps to the front door—a better choice than the kitchen if she hoped to avoid Adam—and stopped dead when he opened it for her. Adam stood back so she could come inside.

"We fell asleep!" she blurted. "Oh, Lord, that came out all wrong! Look, Adam, I can explain everything. Buck and I did fall asleep, but we weren't sleeping together!"

"I wouldn't have let you sleep, either," he drawled. "Not when there are so many more interesting things to do with the time."

"I mean, we didn't have sex," she said, irritated by his sarcasm.

"Oh, really?" It was obvious he didn't believe her.

"I'm telling you the truth!"

"What makes you think I care who you spent the night with, or what you did?" he said in a voice that could have cut steel.

"I'm telling you that absolutely nothing sexual happened between me and Buck Magnesson last night," she insisted.

Adam wanted to believe her. But he couldn't imagine how Buck could have kept her out all night and not have touched her. He didn't have that kind of willpower himself. His mouth was opened and the words were out before he knew he was going to say them.

"I made you an offer once, *little girl,* and I meant it. If you're looking for more experience in bed, I'll be more than happy to provide it."

Tate's eyes widened as she realized what Adam's harsh-sounding words really meant. He was *jealous!* He *did* care! If only there was some way of provoking him into admitting how he really felt! Of course, there was something that might work. It was an outrageous idea, but then, as her brother Faron had always preached, "A faint heart never filled a flush."

Tate sat down on the brass-studded leather sofa and pulled off one of her boots. When Adam said nothing, she pulled off the other one. Then she stood up and began releasing the zipper down the side of her skirt.

"What are you doing?" he asked at last.

"I'm taking you up on your offer."

"What? Are you serious?"

"Absolutely! Weren't you?" She looked up at him coyly, batted her lashes, and had the satisfaction of seeing him flush.

"You don't know what you're doing," he said.

"I know exactly what I'm doing," she replied.

Her skirt landed in a pile at her feet, and Tate was left standing in a frilly slip and a peasant blouse that was well on its way to falling off her shoulder.

Adam swallowed hard. He knew he ought to stop her, but was powerless to do so. "Maria will be—"

"You know Maria isn't here. Sunday is her day off."

Tate reached for the hem of her blouse and pulled it up over her head.

Adam gasped. He had never seen her in a bra before—if that's what you called the tiny piece of confection that hugged her breasts and offered them up in lacy cups for a hungry man's palate.

Tate watched Adam's pulse jump when she stepped out of the circle of her skirt and walked toward him. His hand was warm when she took it in her own. "Your bedroom or mine?" she asked.

"Mine," he croaked.

Adam allowed himself to be led to his bedroom as though he had no will of his own. Indeed, he felt as though he were living some sort of fantasy. Since it was one very much to his liking, he wasn't putting up much of a struggle—none, actually—to be free.

"Here we are," Tate said as she closed the door behind her, shutting them into Adam's bedroom alone.

"I've never been made love to in the morning," Tate said. "Is there any special way it should be done?"

What healthy, red-blooded male could resist that kind of invitation?

Adam swept Tate off her feet. From then on she was caught up in a whirlwind of passion that left her breathless and panting. But now he led and she followed.

Lips reached out for lips. Flesh reached out for flesh. She was aware of textures, hard and soft, silky and crisp, rigid and supple, as Adam introduced her to the delights of sex in the warm sunlight.

This time there was no pain, only joy as he joined their bodies and made them one. When it was over, they lay together in the tangled sheets, her head on his shoulder, his hand on her hip, in a way that spoke volumes about the true state of their hearts.

Tate was aware of the fact Adam hadn't said a word since she had closed the bedroom door behind them. She didn't want to break the magic spell, so she remained silent. But it was plain from the way Adam began moving restlessly, tugging on the sheet, rearranging it to cover and uncover various parts of her body, that there was something he wanted to get off his chest.

"I don't want you to go out with Buck anymore," he said in a quiet voice.

"All right."

"Just like that? All right?"

"I don't want Buck," she said. "I want you."

Adam groaned and pulled her into his arms, holding her so tightly that she protested, "I'm not going anywhere!"

"I can hardly believe that you're here. That you want to be here," Adam said with a boyish grin. "I've been going crazy for the past week."

"Me, too," Tate admitted. "But everything is going to be perfect now, isn't it, Adam? You do love me, don't you?"

She didn't wait for an answer, just kept on talking.

"We can be married and start a family. Oh, how I'd love to have a little boy with your blue eyes and—"

Adam abruptly sat up on the edge of the bed.

Tate put a hand on his back and he shrugged it off. "Adam? What's wrong?"

He looked over his shoulder with eyes as desolate as an endless desert. "I thought I'd made it clear that I wasn't offering marriage."

"But you love me. Don't you?"

Instead of replying to her question, he said, "I was married once before, for eight years. It ended in a bitter divorce. I have no desire to repeat the experience."

Tate couldn't have been more shocked if Adam had said he was a convicted mass murderer. "Why didn't you ever say anything to me about this before?"

"It wasn't any of your business."

"Well, now it is!" she retorted, stung by his bluntness. "You don't have to make the same mistakes this time around, Adam. Just because one marriage failed doesn't mean another will."

He clenched his teeth, trying to dredge up the courage to tell her the truth. But he wasn't willing to risk the possibility that she would choose having children over having him. And he refused to offer marriage while his awful secret lay like a wedge between them.

"I want you in my bed, I won't deny it," Adam said. "But you'll have to settle for what I'm offering."

"What's that?" Tate asked. "An affair?"

Adam shrugged. "If you want to call it that."

"And when you're tired of me, then what?"

I'll never get tired of you. "We'll cross that river when we get to it."

Tate was shaken by the revelation that Adam had been married. She wished she knew more about what had gone wrong to make him sound so bitter. Her pride urged her to leave while she still could. But her heart couldn't face a future that didn't include Adam. With the naïveté of youth, she still believed that love would conquer all, that somehow, everything would work out and that they would live happily ever after.

"All right," she said at last. "An affair it is."

She snuggled up to Adam's back. He took her arms and pulled them around his chest.

"It's a good thing my brothers can't see me now," she teased.

"I'd be a dead man for sure," he said with a groan.

"Just thank your lucky stars that I've been using a false last name. They'll never find me here."

"Let's hope not," Adam muttered.

The conversation ended there, because Adam turned and pulled Tate around onto his lap. He still didn't quite believe that she hadn't stalked out in high dudgeon, that she had chosen to stay. He straightened her legs around his lap and slipped inside her.

Tate learned yet another way to make love in the morning.

It was a mere three weeks later that their idyll came to a shocking and totally unforeseen end.

Chapter 8

TATE WAS PREGNANT. At least she thought she was. She was sitting in Dr. Kowalski's office, waiting for her name to be called so she could find out if the results of her home pregnancy test were as accurate as the company claimed. She was only eight days late, but never once had such a phenomenon occurred in the past. Who would have thought you could get pregnant the first time out!

It had to have happened then, because after that first time she had gone to see Dr. Kowalski and been fitted for a diaphragm. She had managed to use it every time she had made love with Adam over the past three weeks—except the time she had seduced him after spending the night at the river with Buck. So maybe it had happened the second time out. That was beginner's luck for you!

"Mrs. Whitelaw? You're next."

Tate sat up, then realized the nurse had said *Mrs.* Whitelaw. Besides, she had given her name as Tate Whatly. So who was this mysterious *Mrs.* Whitelaw?

The tall woman who stood up was very pregnant. The condition obviously agreed with her, because her skin glowed with health. She had curly blond hair that fell to her shoulders and a face that revealed her age and character in smile lines at the edges of her cornflower-blue eyes and the parentheses bracketing her mouth.

Tate found it hard to believe that it was pure coincidence that this woman had the same unusual last name as she did. Jesse had been gone for so long without any word that Tate immediately began weaving fantasies around the pregnant woman. Maybe this was Jesse's wife. Maybe Jesse would walk in that door in a few minutes and Tate would see him at long last.

Maybe pigs would fly.

Tate watched the woman disappear into an examining room. She was left with little time to speculate because she was called next.

"Ms. Whatly?"

"Uh, yes." She had almost forgotten the phony name she had given the nurse.

"You can come on back now. We'll need a urine specimen, and then I'd like you to strip down and put on this gown. It ties in front. The doctor will be with you in a few minutes."

Tate had had only one pelvic examination in her life— when she had been fitted for the diaphragm—and all the medical hardware attached to the examining table looked as cold and intimidating as she remembered. The wait seemed more like an hour, but actually was only about fifteen minutes. Tate had worked herself into a pretty good case of nerves by the time Dr. Kowalski came into the room.

"Hello, Tate. I understand the rabbit died."

The doctor's teasing smile and her twinkling eyes immediately put Tate at ease. "I'm afraid so," she answered.

The doctor's hands were as warm as her manner. Tate found herself leaving the doctor's office a short time later with a prescription for prenatal vitamins and another appointment in six weeks.

Tate was in the parking lot, still dazed by the confirmation of the fact she was going to have Adam's baby, when she realized that the woman who had been identified as Mrs. Whitelaw was trying to hoist her ungainly body into a pickup.

Tate hurried over to her. "Need a hand?"

"I think I can manage," the woman answered with a friendly smile. "Thanks, anyway."

Tate closed the door behind the pregnant woman, then cupped her hands over the open window frame. "The nurse called you Mrs. Whitelaw. Would you by any chance know a Jesse Whitelaw?"

The woman smiled again. "He's my husband."

Tate's jaw dropped. "No fooling! Really? Jesse's your husband! You've got to be kidding! Why, that means he's going to be a father!"

The woman chuckled at Tate's exuberance. "He sure is. My name's Honey," the woman said. "What's yours?"

"I'm Tate. Wow! This is fantastic! I can't believe this! Wait until I tell Faron and Garth!"

Tate sobered suddenly. She couldn't contact Faron and Garth to tell them she had found Jesse without taking the chance of having them discover her whereabouts. But Jesse wouldn't know she had run away from home. She could see him, and share this joy with him.

With the mention of Tate's name, and then Faron's and Garth's, Honey's gaze had become speculative, and finally troubled. When Honey had first found out she was pregnant, she had urged Jesse to get back in touch with his family. It had taken a little while to convince him, but eventually she had.

When Jesse had called Hawk's Way, he had found his brothers frantic with worry. His little sister Tate had disappeared from the face of the earth, and Faron and Garth feared she had suffered some dire fate.

If Honey wasn't mistaken, she was looking at her husband's little sister—the one who had been missing for a good two and a half months. The prescription for prenatal vitamins that Tate had been waving in her hand suggested that Jesse's little sister had been involved in a few adventures since she had left home.

"I have a confession to make," Tate said, interrupting Honey's thoughts. "Jesse—your husband—is my brother! That makes us sisters, I guess. Gee, I never had a sister. This is great!"

Honey smiled again at Tate's ebullience. "Maybe you'd like to come home with me and see Jesse," she offered.

Tate's brow furrowed as she tried to imagine what Jesse's reaction would be to the fact that she was here on her own. On second thought, it might be safer to meet him on her own ground. "Why don't you and Jesse come over for dinner at my place instead?" Tate said.

"Your place?"

Tate grinned and said, "Well, it's not exactly *mine*. I'm living at the Lazy S and working as a bookkeeper for Adam Philips."

"Horsefeathers," Honey murmured.

"Is something wrong?"

"No. Nothing." Except that Adam Philips was the man she had jilted to marry Jesse Whitelaw.

"Well, do you think you could come?"

If Tate didn't realize the can of worms she was opening, Honey wasn't about to be the one to tell her. Honey was afraid that if she didn't take advantage of Tate's offer, the girl might run into Jesse sometime when Honey wasn't around. From facts Honey knew—that Tate obviously didn't—it was clear the fur was going to fly. Honey wanted to be there to make sure everyone came out with a whole skin.

"Of course we'll come," she said. "What time?"

"About seven. See you then, Honey. Oh, and it was nice meeting you."

"Nice meeting you, too," Honey murmured as Tate turned and hurried away. Honey watched the younger woman yank open the door to the '51 Chevy pickup her brothers claimed she had confiscated when she had run away from home.

"Horsefeathers," she said again. The word didn't do nearly enough to express the foreboding she felt about the evening ahead of her.

Meanwhile, Tate was floating on air. This was going to work out perfectly. She would introduce Adam to her brother and his wife, and later, when they were alone, she would tell Adam that he was going to be a father.

Boy was he going to be surprised!

Tate refused to imagine Adam's reaction as anything other than ecstatic. After all, just as two people didn't have to be married to have sex, they didn't have to be married to have children, either. After all, lots of movie stars were doing it. Why couldn't they?

Long before seven o'clock Tate heard someone pounding

on the front door. She knew it couldn't be the company she had invited, and from the sound of things it was an emergency. She ran to open the door and gasped when she realized who was standing there.

"Jesse!"

"So it *is* you!"

Tate launched herself into her brother's arms. He lifted her up and swung her in a circle, just as he had the last time they had seen each other, when she was a child of eight.

Jesse looked so much the same, and yet he was different. His dark eyes were still as fierce as ever, his black hair still as shaggy. But his face was lined, and his body that of a mature man, not the twenty-year-old boy who had gone away when she was just a little girl.

"You look wonderful, Tate," Jesse said.

"So do you," she said with an irrepressible grin. She angled her head around his broad chest, trying to locate Honey. "Where's your wife?"

"I came ahead of her." Actually, he had snuck out behind Honey's back and come running to save his little sister from that sonofabitch Adam Philips. Jesse had never liked the man, and now his feelings had been vindicated. Just look how Philips had taken advantage of his baby sister!

"Faron and Garth have been worried to death about you," Jesse chastised.

"You've been in touch with them? When? How?"

"Honey talked me into calling them when she found out for sure she was pregnant. Is it true what Honey told me? Are you living here with Adam Philips?" Jesse demanded.

"I work here," Tate said, the pride she felt in her job apparent in her voice. "I'm Adam's bookkeeper."

"What else do you do for Adam?"

Tate hissed in a breath of air. "I don't think I like your tone of voice."

"Get your things," Jesse ordered. "You're getting out of here."

Tate's hands fisted and found her hips. "I left home to get away from that kind of high-handedness. I don't intend to let you get away with it, either," she said tartly. "I happen to enjoy my job, and I have no intention of giving it up."

"You don't have any idea what can happen to a young woman living alone with a man!"

"Oh, don't I?"

"Do you mean to say that you and Philips—"

"My relationship with Adam is no concern of yours."

Jesse's dark eyes narrowed speculatively. His little sister glowed from the inside out. He was mentally adding one and one— and getting three. "Honey said she met you in the parking lot of Doc Kowalski's office, but she didn't say what you were doing there. What were you doing there, Tate? Are you sick?"

Jesse was just fishing, Tate thought. He couldn't know anything for sure. But even a blind pig will find an acorn once in a while. She had to do something to distract him.

"Honey's a really beautiful woman, Jesse. How did you meet her?"

"Don't change the subject, Tate."

Jesse had just grabbed Tate by the arm when Adam stepped into the living room from the kitchen. "I thought I heard voices in here." Adam spied Jesse's hold on Tate, and his body tensed. He welcomed the long overdue confrontation with

Tate's brother. "Hello, Jesse. Would you mind telling me what's going on?"

"I'm taking my sister home," Jesse said.

Adam searched Tate's face, looking deep into her hazel eyes. "Is that what you want?"

"I want to stay here."

"You heard her, Jesse," Adam said in a steely voice. "Let her go."

"You bastard! It'll be a cold day in hell before I leave my sister in your clutches."

Adam took a step forward, eyes flashing, teeth bared, fists clenched.

"Stop it! Both of you!" Tate yanked herself free from Jesse's grasp, but remained between the two men, a human barrier to the violence that threatened to erupt at any moment.

"Get out of the way, Tate," Jesse said.

"Do as he says," Adam ordered.

Tate put a firm, flat palm on each man's chest to keep them apart. "I said stop it, and I meant it!"

"I'm taking you home, Tate," Jesse said. But his words and the challenge were meant for Adam.

"If Tate wants to stay, she stays!" Adam retorted, accepting the summons to battle.

Tate might as well not have been there for as much attention either man paid to her. She was merely the prize to be won. They were intent only on the conflict to come.

There was a loud knocking at the door, but before any of them could move, it opened and Honey stepped inside. "Thank goodness I got here in time!"

Honey stepped between the two men who fell back in deference to her pregnant state. "What are you two doing to this poor girl?" She slipped a comforting arm around Tate's shoulder. "Are you all right, Tate?"

"I'm fine," Tate said. "But these two idiots are about to start pounding on each other!"

"He's got it coming!" Jesse growled. "What kind of low-down hyena seduces an innocent child!"

"Jesse!" Tate cried, mortified as much by his use of the term *child* as by his accusation. Jesse might still remember her as a child, but she was a woman now.

Adam's face had bleached white. "You're way off base, Whitelaw," he snarled.

"Can you say you aren't sleeping with her?" Jesse demanded.

"That's none of your damn business!" Adam snapped back.

Honey stepped back a pace, taking Tate with her, beyond the range of the animosity radiating from the two powerful men.

Tate turned to plead peace with her brother. "I love Adam," she said.

"But I'll bet he hasn't said he loves you," Jesse retorted in a mocking voice.

Tate lowered her eyes and bit her lip.

"I thought not!" he said triumphantly.

Tate's chin lifted and her eyes flashed defiance. "I won't leave him!"

"He's just using you to get back at me," Jesse said. "The reason I know he can't love you, is because *I* stole the woman *he* wanted right out from under his nose."

"What?" Confused, Tate looked from her brother to her lover. Adam's eyes were dark with pain and regret.

Tate whirled her head to look at Honey. The pregnant

woman's arms were folded protectively around her unborn child. Her cheeks flamed. She slowly lifted her lids and allowed Tate to see the guilt in her lovely cornflower-blue eyes.

It couldn't be true! Adam wouldn't have done something so heinous as to seduce her to get back at her brother for stealing the woman he loved. But none of the three parties involved was denying it.

Her eyes sought out Adam's face again, looking for some shred of hope that her brother was lying. "Adam?"

Adam's stony features spoke volumes even though he remained mute.

"Oh, God," Tate breathed. "This can't be happening to me!"

Jesse lashed out with his fist at the man who had caused his sister so much pain. Adam instinctively stepped back and Jesse's fist swung through empty air. Before Jesse could swing the other fist, Honey had thrown herself in front of her husband.

"Please don't fight! Please, Jesse!"

It was a tribute to how much Jesse loved his wife that he held himself in check. He circled his wife's shoulder with one hand and held out the other to Tate.

"Are you coming?" he asked.

"I…I'm staying." At least until she had a chance to talk with Adam in private and hear his side of this unbelievable story. Then she would decide whether to tell him that she was going to have his child.

Honey saw that her husband was ready to argue further and intervened. "She's a grown woman, Jesse. She has to make her own choices."

"Dammit, this is the wrong one!" Jesse snarled.

"But it is my choice," Tate said in a quiet voice.

Honey slipped her arm around her husband's waist. "Let's go home, Jesse."

"I'm leaving," Jesse said. "But I'll be back with Faron and Garth." He yanked open the door, urged his wife out of the house and quickly followed, slamming the door after him.

Tate felt her stomach fall to her feet. She had been surprised to see Adam stand up to her brother—overjoyed, in fact. But if all three of the Whitelaw brothers showed up, there was no way Adam would be able to endure against them. Her brothers would haul her back home before she had time to say yeah, boo, or "I'm pregnant."

"You might as well say goodbye to me now," she said glumly. "When Faron and Garth find out where I am they'll be coming for me."

"No one—your brothers included—is going to take you from the Lazy S if you don't want to go," Adam said in a hard voice.

"Does that mean you want me to stay?"

Adam nodded curtly.

She didn't want to ask, but she had to. "Is it true, what my brother said? Did you love Honey?"

That same curt nod in response.

Tate felt the constriction in her chest tighten. "Would you have married her if Jesse hadn't come along?"

Adam shoved a hand through his hair in agitation. "I don't know. I wanted to marry her. I'm not so sure she was as anxious to marry me. I asked her. She never said yes."

That was small comfort to Tate, who was appalled to hear how close Adam had come to marrying her brother's wife.

"Is that why you can't love me?" Tate asked. "Because you're still in love with her?"

The tortured look of pain on Adam's face left Tate feeling certain she had hit upon the truth. But she didn't despair. In fact, she felt a great deal of hope. Adam must realize that he could never have Honey Whitelaw now. Time was the best doctor for a wound of the heart. And time was on her side.

She very carefully did not bring up the subject of Jesse's accusation that Adam had made love to her to get revenge on her brother. In her heart she knew Adam would never use her like that. He might not be able to say he loved her—yet—but she was certain that one day he would.

"I need a hug," Tate said.

Adam opened his arms and Tate stepped into them. She snuggled against him, letting the love she felt flow over them both. But his body remained stiff and unyielding.

"Adam, I'm…" The word *pregnant* wouldn't come out.

"What is it, Tate?"

His voice sounded harsh in her ear, his tone still as curt as the abrupt nods with which he had acknowledged his love for another woman. Maybe Tate would just wait a little while before she told him she was carrying his child.

"I'm glad you want me to stay," she said.

He hugged her harder, until his hold was almost painful. Tate felt tears pool in the corners of her eyes. She blamed the phenomenon now on the heightened emotions caused by her pregnancy.

But the devil on her shoulder forced her to admit that unsettling seeds of doubt had been planted concerning whether everything would turn out happily ever after.

Chapter 9

TATE SPENT THE NIGHT in Adam's arms. He couldn't have been more comforting. But for the first time since they had begun sleeping together, they didn't make love.

When they met across the kitchen table the next morning, an awkwardness existed between them that had not been there in the past.

"You must eat more, *señorita*," Maria urged. "You will not make it through the day on so little."

"I'm not hungry," Tate said. Actually, she had already snuck in earlier and had a light breakfast to stave off the first symptoms of morning sickness. Under Maria's stern eye, she dutifully applied herself to the bowl of oatmeal in front of her.

Tate's concentration was so complete that she paid no attention to the subsequent conversation Maria conducted with Adam in Spanish.

"The *señorita* has been crying," Maria said.

Adam glanced at Tate's red-rimmed eyes. "Her brother came to visit yesterday, the one she hasn't seen since she was a child."

"This brother made her cry?"

"He wanted her to go away with him."

"Ah. But you did not let her go."

"She chose to stay," Adam corrected.

"Then why was she crying?" Maria asked.

A muscle worked in Adam's jaw. At last he answered, "Because she's afraid I don't love her."

"Stupid man! Why don't you tell her so and put the smile back on her face?"

Adam sighed disgustedly. "I don't think she'll believe me now."

Maria shook her head and clucked her tongue. "I am going to the store to buy groceries. I will not be coming back for two—no, three hours. Tell her you love her."

Adam's lips curled sardonically. "All right, Maria. I'll give it a try."

Tate had been making shapes with her oatmeal and had only eaten about three bites when Maria whisked the bowl out from in front of her.

"I need to clear the table so I can go shopping," Maria said. She refilled Tate's coffee cup. "You sit here and enjoy another cup of coffee."

She refilled Adam's cup as well and, giving him a suggestive look, said, "You keep the *señorita* company."

Maria took off her apron, picked up her purse and left by the kitchen door a few moments later.

When she was gone, the silence seemed oppressive. Finally Adam said, "What are your plans for today?"

"I guess I'll input some more information on the computer. What about you?"

"I'm moving cattle from one pasture to another."

"Your job sounds like more fun than mine. Can I come along?"

"I don't think that would be a good idea."

"Oh."

Adam saw the look on Tate's face and realized she thought he was rejecting her—again. He swore under his breath. "Look, Tate. I think we'd better have a talk."

Tate rose abruptly. This was where Adam told her that he had thought things over and he wanted her to leave the Lazy S after all. She wasn't going to hang around to let him do it. "I'd better get going. I—"

Adam caught her before she had gone two steps. He took her shoulders in his hands, turning her to face him. She kept her eyes lowered, refusing to look at him.

"Tate," he said in a voice that was tender with the love he felt for her. "Look at me."

Her eyes were more green than gold. He couldn't bear to see the sadness in them. He grasped her nape and pulled her toward him as his mouth lowered to claim hers.

It was a hungry kiss. A kiss of longing for things that ought to be. A kiss fierce with passion. And tender with love.

Adam wanted to be closer. He pulled her T-shirt up and over her head, then yanked the snaps open down the front of his shirt and pulled the tails out of his jeans. He sighed in satisfaction as he closed his arms around her and snuggled her naked breasts tight against his chest.

"Lord, sweetheart. You feel so good!" He cupped her fanny with his hands and lifted her, rubbing himself against her, letting the layers of denim add to the friction between them.

His mouth found a spot beneath her ear that he knew was sensitive, and he sucked just hard enough to make her moan with pleasure.

Adam froze when he heard the kitchen door being flung open. He whirled to meet whatever threat was there, pulling Tate close and pressing her face against his chest protectively.

Tate felt Adam's body tense, felt his shoulders square and his stance widen. She knew who it was, who it had to be. She turned her head. There in the doorway stood her three brothers, Faron, Jesse and Garth. And Garth was carrying a shotgun.

Tate felt her face flush to the roots of her hair. She was naked from the waist up, and there could be no doubt as to what she had been doing with Adam. Or, from the looks on their faces, how her brothers felt about it. She closed her eyes and clutched Adam, knowing her brothers planned to tear them apart.

"Make yourself decent!" Garth ordered.

Tate reached across to the chair where Adam had slung her T-shirt, and with her back to her brothers, pulled it over her head. When she turned to face them, Adam put an arm around her waist and pulled her snug against his hip.

The three men crowded into the kitchen. It soon became apparent they hadn't come alone. An elderly gentleman wearing a clerical collar and carrying what Tate supposed to be a Bible followed them inside.

"You have a choice," Garth said to Adam. "You can make an honest woman of my sister, or I can kill you."

Adam cocked a brow. "That's murder."

Garth smiled grimly. "It'll be an accidental shooting, of course."

"Of course," Adam said, his lips twisting cynically. "What if Tate and I aren't ready to get married?"

"Man gets a woman pregnant, it's time to marry her," Jesse snarled. "I made a point of seeing Doc Kowalski on the way home last night and told her Tate was my sister. She congratulated me on the fact I'll soon be an *uncle!*"

Adam froze. He turned to stare at Tate, but she refused to meet his gaze. His hand tightened on her waist. "Are you pregnant, Tate?"

She nodded.

Adam's lips flattened and a muscle worked in his jaw. He grabbed hold of her chin and forced it up. "Whose child is it? Buck's?"

"Yours!" Tate cried, jerking her head from his grasp.

"Not mine," he said flatly. "I'm sterile."

Tate sank into a kitchen chair at one end of the table, her eyes never wavering from Adam's granitelike expression.

Meanwhile, Tate's brothers were in a quandary.

"We can't force him to marry Tate if the child's not his," Faron argued.

"But it must be his!" Jesse said. "Look how we found them today!"

Garth handed the shotgun to Faron, then crossed and sat down beside Tate on the opposite side of the table from Adam. He took Tate's hand from her lap and held it in his for a moment, gently rubbing her knuckles. "I want you to be honest with me, Tate. Have you been with another man besides Adam?"

"No! I'm carrying Adam's child, whether he believes it or not!"

"Adam says he's sterile," Garth persisted.

"I don't care what he says," Tate said through clenched teeth. "I'm telling the truth."

Garth and Faron exchanged a significant glance. Garth stood and confronted Adam. "Can you deny you've made love to my sister?"

"No, I don't deny that."

"Then my original offer still holds," Garth said.

"Given that choice, I suppose I have no choice," Adam conceded with a stony glare.

"What about me?" Tate asked. "Don't I get a choice?"

"You'll do as you're told," Garth commanded. "Or else."

"Or else what?"

"You come home to Hawk's Way."

Tate shuddered. There seemed no escape from the ultimatum Garth had given her. At least if she went through with the wedding, she would still have her freedom. Once her brothers had her safely married they would go back where they had come from—and she could figure out what to do from there.

"All right. Let's get this over with," she said.

"Reverend Wheeler, if you please?" Garth directed the minister to the head of the table, arranged Tate and Adam on one side, and stood on the other side with Faron and Jesse.

He told Adam, "I had to cut a few corners, but I've taken care of getting the license." He gestured to the minister. "Whenever you're ready, Reverend."

If Reverend Wheeler hadn't baptized Tate and presided at her confirmation, he might have had some qualms about what he was about to do. Never had bride and bridegroom looked less happy to be wed. But he firmly believed in the sanctity of home and family. And Garth had promised a large donation to build the new Sunday school wing.

The reverend opened the Bible he had brought along and began to read, "Dearly Beloved…"

Tate listened, but she didn't hear what was being said, spoke when called upon, but was unaware of the answers she gave. She had fallen into a deep well of despair.

Tate had never really thought about having a big wedding, but a white T-shirt was a poor substitute for a wedding gown. She wouldn't have minded giving up the festive trappings, if only she were sure the man standing beside her wanted to be her husband.

Adam did not.

How had things gone so wrong? Tate had never meant to trap Adam. It was clear he thought she had slept with Buck, and that the baby wasn't his. She knew from her experience with Buck and Velma that a marriage that lacked trust—on both sides—was in deep trouble. If Adam believed she had lied about the child's father, wouldn't he expect her to lie about other things? Would he, like Buck, overreact from now on if she so much as looked at another man? Of course Buck was jealous because he loved Velma. Tate wasn't so sure about Adam's feelings. He had never once said he loved her.

Tate would have given anything if she had just told Adam about the baby last night. Then, they would have had a chance to discuss things alone. Such as why a man who was obviously able to sire children thought he was sterile.

"Tate?"

"What?"

"Hold out your hand so Adam can put the ring on your finger," Garth said.

What ring? Tate thought.

"With this ring I thee wed," Adam said. He slipped the turquoise ring he usually wore on his little finger on the third finger of Tate's left hand.

Tate was lost. What had happened to the rest of the ceremony? Had she said "I do"?

Reverend Wheeler said, "I now pronounce you man and wife. You may kiss the bride."

When neither of the newlyweds moved, Faron said in a quiet—some might have said gentle—voice, "It's time to kiss your bride now, Adam."

Adam wanted to refuse. It was all a sham, anyway. But when Tate turned her face up to him she looked so bewildered he felt the urge to take her in his arms and protect her.

Garth cleared his throat at the delay.

Adam's jaw tightened. Tate already had three very efficient guardians. She didn't need him. But he found himself unable to resist the temptation of her lips, still swollen from his earlier kisses. Her eyes slid closed as he lowered his head. He touched his lips lightly to hers, taking the barest taste of her with the tip of his tongue.

If this had been a real wedding he would have wanted to cherish this moment. From the shuffling sounds across the table, Adam was reminded that it was real enough. So he took what he wanted from Tate, ravaging her mouth, letting her feel his fury and frustration at what her brothers had robbed them of when they had insisted on this forced marriage.

As soon as he lifted his head Adam saw that Garth had crossed around the table. Instead of the punch in the nose Adam expected, Tate's oldest brother held out his hand to be shaken. To Adam's further surprise, Garth had a grin on his face.

"Welcome to the family," Garth said. He gave Tate a fierce hug. "Be happy!" he whispered in her ear.

Faron was next to shake Adam's hand. "How about a drink

to celebrate?" he asked. "I've got champagne on ice outside in the pickup."

"I guess that would be all right," Adam said, still stunned by the abrupt change in attitude of Tate's brothers.

Faron headed outside as Jesse approached Adam. The two men eyed each other warily.

At last Jesse held out his hand. "Truce?"

When Adam hesitated, Jesse said, "Honey will kill me if we don't make peace." When Adam still hesitated, Jesse added, "For Tate's sake?"

Adam shook hands with Tate's middle brother. They would never be good friends. But they were neighbors, and now brothers-in-law. For their wives' sakes, they would tolerate one another.

The wedding celebration was a lively affair. Now that Adam had done the right thing by Tate, her brothers were more than willing to treat him like one of the family.

As the morning wore on and Adam had a few glasses of champagne—and more than a few glasses of whiskey—he began to think maybe things hadn't turned out so badly after all.

Now that he and Tate were married, there was no reason why they couldn't make the best of the situation. He couldn't feel sorry about the baby, even if it meant Tate had lied to him about sleeping with Buck. He had always wanted children, and this one would be especially beloved because it would belong to him and Tate.

After he made love to his wife, Adam would tell her that he loved her. They could forget what had happened in the past. Their lives could begin from there.

Tate's brothers might have stayed longer, except Honey called to make sure everything had turned out all right. When

Jesse hung up the phone, he said to his brothers, "I know you don't want to be reminded, but I have work that has to get done today."

Faron guffawed and said, "Tell the truth. What you're really concerned about is getting home to your wife."

The three brothers kidded each other good-naturedly all the way out the door. Once they and the preacher were gone, Tate closed the door and leaned her forehead against the cool wood frame.

"I'm sorry, Adam."

He crossed to her and slipped his arms around her waist from behind. "It's all right, Tate. It wasn't your fault."

"They're *my* brothers."

"They only did what they thought was best for you." Despite the fact he was a victim of their manipulation, Adam could sympathize with her brothers. If Melanie had lived…if he had found her in the same circumstances…he might have done the same thing. And hoped for the best. As Adam was hoping for the best now with Tate.

He kissed her nape and felt her shiver in his arms. "Come to bed, Tate. It's our wedding day."

She kept her face pressed to the door. She was too intent on giving Adam back his freedom to hear the message of love in his words and his caress. "I can't stand it—knowing you were trapped into marrying me." She felt his body stiffen, and said, "I promise I'll give you a divorce. As soon as the baby is born I—"

Adam grabbed her by the arm and jerked her around to face him. "Is that the reason you agreed to marry me? So you can have a name for your bastard?"

"Please, Adam—"

"Don't beg, Tate, it doesn't become you."

Tate had slapped him before she was aware she had raised her hand. She gasped when she saw the stark imprint her fingers had left on his cheek.

Adam grabbed her wrist. Tate could feel him trembling with rage. She waited to see what form his retaliation would take.

"All right," Adam said in the harshest voice she had ever heard him use. "I'll give you what you want. Your baby will have my name and you can have your divorce. But there's something I want in return, Tate."

"What?" she breathed.

"You. I want you in my bed every night." His grasp on her wrist tightened. "Warm. And willing. Do I make myself understood?"

Oh, she understood, all right. She had offered him the divorce hoping he would refuse. His ultimatum made it clear what he had wanted from her all along. Well, she would just show him what he was so willing to give up!

"Believe me, you're going to get what you're asking for, Adam," she said in a silky voice. *And a whole lot more!*

He started for the bedroom, his hand firmly clamped around her wrist. Tate hurried to catch up, afraid that if she fell, he would simply drag her behind him.

When they arrived in the bedroom he closed the door behind her. Only then did he release her. "Get undressed," he ordered. He crossed his arms and stood there, legs widespread, staring at her.

Tate held herself proudly erect. Sooner or later Adam was going to realize the truth. The child she carried was his. Meanwhile, he was going to get every bit of what he had demanded—and perhaps even more than he had bargained for.

Tate had never stripped to tease a man. She did so now.

The T-shirt came off first. Slowly. She let it hang by one finger for a moment before it dropped to the floor. She looked down at her breasts and saw the aureoles were pink and full. She reached down to brush her fingertips across her nipples, then returned to tease the pink buds until they stood erect.

Adam hissed in a breath of air.

Tate didn't dare look at him, afraid she would lose her nerve. Instead she smoothed her hands over her belly and down across the delta of her thighs, spreading her legs so that her hand could cup the heat there. She glided her hands back up the length of her body, feeling the textures of her skin, aware of the prickles as her flesh responded to the knowledge that Adam was watching every move she made.

She shoved her hands into her hair at the temples and then gathered her hair and lifted it off her nape, knowing that as she raised her arms her breasts would follow. She arched her back in a sensuous curve that thrust breasts and belly toward Adam.

She actually heard him swallow. Then she made the mistake of looking at him—at his bare chest. His nipples were as turgid as hers. As she relaxed her body into a more natural pose, she met blue eyes so dark with passion they were more the hue of a stormy sky.

His nostrils were flared to drink in the scent of her. His body was wired taut as a bowstring, fists clenched at his sides. His manhood was a hard ridge that threatened the seams at the crotch of his jeans. As his tongue reached out to lick at the perspiration on his upper lip, she felt her groin tighten with answering pleasure.

Tate felt exultant. Powerful. And oh, so much a woman. Encouraged by her success, she reached down for the snap of her jeans. Adam's whole body jerked when it popped free. The rasp of her zipper as she slid it down was matched by the harsh sound of Adam's breathing.

She slowly turned down each side of her jeans in front, creating a V through which the white of her panties showed. Then she spread her legs, stuck her thumbs into her panties and let her fingers slide down inside the jeans, pulling her underwear down and slowly exposing a V of flesh on her belly.

Adam swore under his breath. But he didn't move an inch.

Tate took a deep breath and shoved both panties and jeans down low on her hips, revealing her hipbones and belly and a hint of dark curls at the crest of her thighs. She put her hands behind her and rubbed her buttocks, easing the jeans down a little more with each circular motion.

She stuck her thumbs back in the front of the jeans, and met Adam's gaze before skimming her fingers across her pubic arch. A pulse in his temple jumped. His jaw clenched. But otherwise he didn't stir from where he was standing.

Tate smiled, a feminine smile of enjoyment and satisfaction. She gave one last little shove and both panties and jeans began the slide down to her ankles, where she stepped out of jeans, panties and moccasins all at once.

At last Tate stood naked before Adam. Her body felt languid, graceful as it never had. She realized it was because Adam adored her with his eyes. Because he desired her with his body. She made no move to hide herself from him.

It wasn't until she took a step toward him that Adam finally moved.

He glided toward her like a stalking tiger. Tate felt the sexual energy radiating from him long before their bodies met.

His kiss was fierce, consuming. His hands seemed to be everywhere, touching, demanding a response. She arched against him, feeling the swollen heat and hardness beneath the denim.

Adam didn't bother taking her to bed. He backed her up against the wall, unsnapped his jeans to free himself, then lifted her legs around him and thrust himself inside.

Tate clung to Adam's neck with her arms and to his hips with her legs. His mouth sought hers, and his tongue thrust in rhythm with his body. His hand slipped between them and sought out the tiny nubbin that was the source of her pleasure. His thumb caressed her until he felt the waves of pleasure tightening her inner muscles around him. He threw his head back in ecstasy as his own powerful orgasm spilled inside her.

Then his head fell forward against her shoulder as he struggled to regain his breath. He finally released her legs so that she could stand, but found he had to hold her to keep her from falling, her knees were so wobbly. He lifted her into his arms and carried her to bed, throwing the sheets back and setting her down gently before joining her there.

He pulled the covers up over them both and found he could barely keep his eyes open. But there was something he wanted to say before he fell asleep.

"Tate? Are you awake?"

"Mmm. I guess so," she murmured against his throat.

"You can admit the truth about sleeping with Buck. It isn't going to make a difference in how I feel about you." *Or the baby,* he thought.

Tate pushed herself upright. The sheet that had covered her fell to her waist. "I'm telling the truth, Adam, when I say I never slept with Buck. Why won't you believe me?"

Adam levered himself up on his elbow and met her gaze with a flinty one of his own. "Because I have the medical tests to prove you wrong."

"Then your tests are mistaken!" Tate retorted. She leaned back against the headboard and yanked the covers up to her neck.

Tate had never looked more beautiful. Adam had to lie back and put his hands behind his head to keep from reaching for her again. The three hours Maria had promised to stay gone were nearly up, and he had no doubt the housekeeper would come looking for him to find out whether he had told Tate that he loved her.

He was glad now that he hadn't. At least he had been spared the humbling experience of confessing his love to a woman who had married him only to have a name for her child. Adam lay there trying to figure out why Tate persisted in lying about the baby.

"Does Buck know about the baby?" he asked.

"He guessed," Tate admitted. Buck had known from the glow on her face that something was different and had confronted her about it. She had told him the truth.

"I suppose he refused to marry you because he's still in love with Velma," Adam said.

Tate lurched out of bed and stomped over to where her clothes lay in a pile on the floor. She kept her back to Adam as she began dressing.

"Where are you going?" he asked.

"Anywhere I can be away from you," she retorted.

"Just so long as you stay away from Buck, I don't care—"

Tate whirled and said, "Buck is my friend. I'll see him when and where and as often as I please."

Adam shoved the covers out of the way and yanked on his jeans. "You took vows to me that I don't intend to see you break," he said.

"You're a fool, Adam. You can't see what's right in front of your face."

"I know a whore when I see one."

Adam was sorry the instant the words were out of his mouth. He would have given anything to take them back. He was jealous, and hurt by her apparent devotion to Buck. He had said the first thing that came into his head that he knew would hurt her.

And he was sorry for it. "Tate, I—"

"Don't say anything, Adam. Just get away from me. Maybe someday I'll be able to forgive you for that."

Adam grabbed his shirt, underwear, socks and boots and left the room, closing the door quietly behind him.

Tate sank onto the bed, fighting sobs that made her chest ache. This was worse than anything she had ever imagined. She had ample evidence in Buck's case of how suspicion and mistrust could make a man act irrationally. She had just never expected to see Adam behave like a jealous jackass.

What was she going to do now?

# Chapter 10

ADAM HAD AMPLE TIME all through the day and overnight to regret his outburst. Tate had spent the rest of the day in the office, then retreated to her own bedroom for the night. He had decided it would be best to meet her over the breakfast table and try to mend fences when Maria was there to act as a buffer.

But morning sickness had once again brought Tate to the kitchen early. Instead of waiting to have coffee with Adam, she left the house to go for a walk, hoping it might settle her stomach. Buck waved to her from the loft of the barn, where he was forking down hay. After looking back once at the house, Tate headed toward the barn to talk to him. She had better give him fair warning that Adam was on the warpath and looking for scalps.

Adam's mood wasn't improved when he realized, after sitting at the table for half an hour alone, that Tate wasn't coming to breakfast. He had snapped at Maria like a wounded bear when she started asking questions, and now she wasn't talking to him, either. He shoved his hat down on his head and headed out to the barn to work off some steam by cleaning out stalls.

Adam's eyes had barely adjusted to the shadows in the barn when he spied Tate standing next to the ladder that led to the loft. His heart gave a giant leap—then began to pump with adrenaline when he realized that Buck was standing right beside her. And that the lanky cowboy had his arm around Tate's shoulder.

Adam marched over to Buck and ordered, "Get your hands off my wife."

Buck grinned. "Jealous, huh? You've got no reason—"

Adam thought he had damned good reason to be jealous. After all, his wife was carrying Buck's child. His fist swung hard and fast, straight for Buck's nose.

Buck fell like a stone, his nose squirting blood. Tate quickly knelt beside him, grabbing the bandanna out of her back pocket to staunch the bleeding.

"You idiot!" she snapped at Adam. "Go stick your head in a bucket of water and cool off!"

Adam wanted to yank Tate away from the other man's side, but it was plain he would have a fight on his hands if he tried. His pride wouldn't allow him to ask her nicely to come with him. Not that he could have forced the words past the lump in his throat. "Do as you please," he snarled. "You always have."

With that, he turned and marched right back out of the barn. They heard gravel fly in the drive as he gunned his pickup and drove away.

"Who put a burr under his saddle?" Buck asked, dabbing gently at his nose with the bloody bandanna.

"How did you like the way he treated you?" Tate asked.

"Damn near hated it," Buck replied.

"Think about it the next time you see Velma with another man and decide to take a punch at him. Because that's what an unreasonable, mistrustful, paranoid sonofabitch looks like in action."

Buck's lips quirked at the corners. "Are you saying that's the way I act around Velma?"

"Bingo."

Buck tested the bridge of his nose to see if it were broken. "Maybe this bloody nose wasn't such a bad thing after all."

"Oh?"

"Adam might have knocked some sense into me. I know damn well he has no reason to be jealous, even though he thinks he does. He should have trusted you." Buck struggled to his feet. "Maybe I'll just go see Velma again."

"Is there any chance she'll speak to you?"

"If she's been as miserable as I have the past few weeks, she will," Buck said, a determined light in his brown eyes.

"I wish you luck," Tate said.

"I don't think I'm going to need luck," Buck said. "I've got something even better."

"What's that?"

"I think I just might have had some trust pounded into me."

Tate gave Buck a hug, which he was quick to escape with the excuse of dusting the hay off his britches.

"I may have become a trusting soul," he said, "but Adam's still crazy as a loon. No telling when he'll turn right around and come looking for you. I'd feel a mite safer if you go on back to the house."

Tate did as he asked. She hoped Buck's experience with Adam had shown Buck once and for all the folly of being needlessly jealous. Because if Buck could learn to trust Velma, there was some hope that Adam would one day come to trust her.

Meanwhile, Adam had driven north toward Fredericksburg and was almost into the hill country before he calmed down enough to look around and see where he was. He made a U-turn in the middle of the highway and headed back the way he had come.

Jealousy. Adam had never before had to cope with the feeling, and he had been doing a pretty rotten job of it so far. He could spend the little time he and Tate had together before she sought out a divorce condemning her for what was past. Or he could simply enjoy the company of the irrepressible, lively hoyden he had come to know and love. Between those two choices, the latter made a whole lot more sense.

When Adam arrived back at the ranch house he sought Tate out first in the barn. He found Buck working there.

The lanky cowboy leaned on the pitchfork and said, "You finally come to your senses?"

Adam grinned ruefully. "Yeah. About that punch—"

"Forget it." Buck had been working out how he could use his swollen nose to get Velma's sympathy, and then explain to her the lesson it had taught him. "Believe me, I can understand how you must have felt when you saw me with Tate."

"Because of Velma?" Adam remembered how devastated Buck had been when he had found out his wife was cheating on him.

"Yeah."

"Uh, have you seen Tate?" Adam asked.

"She went back to the house. Look, Adam, you don't—"

"You don't have to explain, Buck. It doesn't matter." Adam turned and headed back to the house. He found Tate working in his office at the computer.

"Busy?"

Tate jumped at the sound of Adam's voice. She looked over her shoulder and found him leaning negligently against the door frame, one hip cocked, his hat in his hands. The anxious way his fingers were working the brim betrayed his nerves.

"Not too busy to talk," she said. She turned the swivel chair in his direction, leaned back, put her ankles on the desk and crossed her arms behind her head. It was a pose intended to be equally carefree. In Tate's case, her bare toes—which wiggled constantly—gave her away.

In his younger days, Adam had ridden bucking broncs in the rodeo. His stomach felt now as it did when he was on the bronc and the chute was about to open. Like the championship rider he was, he gave himself eight good seconds to make his point and get out.

"I'm sorry. I was out of line—with what I said last night and today with Buck. I'm not asking you to forgive me. I'd just like a chance to start over fresh from here."

Tate sat there stunned. *Adam apologizing?* She had never thought she would see the day. But like Velma, once burned, twice chary. "Does this mean you're rescinding the bargain we made?"

Adam swallowed hard. "No."

So, he still wanted her, even though he was convinced the baby was Buck's. And he was willing to keep his mouth shut about her supposed indiscretion—and give his name to Buck's child—in return for favors in bed.

A woman had to be out of her mind to accept a bargain like that.

"All right," Tate said. "I accept your apology. And I agree to abide by the bargain we made yesterday."

Adam noticed she hadn't forgiven him. But then he hadn't

asked for forgiveness. More to the point, she had agreed that their marriage continue to be consummated.

Tate thought she must be an eternal optimist, because she took Adam's appearance at her door as a good sign. She hadn't given up hope that she could somehow convince him of the truth about the baby, and that they would live happily ever after. It might never happen, but at least now they would be living in amity while they tried to work things out.

"It's beautiful out today," Adam said. "How would you like to take a break and come help me? I still have to move those cattle from one pasture to another." Work that hadn't been done yesterday because they had gotten married instead.

A broad smile appeared on Tate's face. "I'd like that. Just let me save this material on the computer."

She dropped her feet and swiveled back around to face the computer. She was interrupted when Adam loudly cleared his throat.

"Uh. I didn't think to ask. Did Dr. Kowalski say everything's okay with the baby? There's no medical reason why you can't do strenuous exercise, is there?"

Tate turned and gave him a beatific smile. "I'm fine. The baby will enjoy the ride."

Nevertheless, Adam kept a close eye on Tate. When he saw her eyelids begin to droop late in the afternoon he suggested they take a siesta. He led her to a giant live oak that stood near the banks of a creek on his property. There he spread a blanket he had tied behind the saddle and provided a picnic he had packed in his saddlebags.

Tate pulled off her boots and wiggled her toes. Then she lay back on the blanket with her hands behind her head and stared up at the freckles of sun visible through the gnarled, moss-laden limbs of the live oak. "This is wonderful! A picnic! I had no idea you had this in mind when you asked me to come with you today."

Actually, Maria was responsible for the impromptu picnic. Adam had thought of the blanket himself. The delight on Tate's face was its own reward. Adam sat down cross-legged across from her and passed out ham and cheese sandwiches, deviled eggs and pickles. There was a thermos of iced tea to drink.

"I don't usually care for pickles," Tate said, crunching into the sweet gherkin in her hand. "But you know, this tastes pretty good."

Adam smiled to himself. In his experience, pregnant women had odd cravings. He had once had a patient who'd eaten liver with peanut butter.

Soon after she had finished her lunch, Tate yawned. "I can't believe how tired I feel lately."

"Your body is going through a lot of changes."

"Is that a medical opinion, Doctor?" Tate asked, eyeing him through half-closed lids. But she didn't hear his answer. The moment she laid her head on her hand and closed her eyes, she fell sound asleep.

Adam cleared away the picnic and lay down beside her to watch her sleep. He had never realized how very long her lashes were, or how very dark. She had a tiny mole beside her ear that he hadn't detected before. And dark circles under her eyes, which he also hadn't noticed.

As a doctor he knew the strain pregnancy put on a woman's body and her emotions. He made a vow to himself to take care of Tate, to make sure that the dark circles disappeared and that the smile stayed on her face.

He knew how she would resent it if she thought he had taken on the role of caretaker. After all, she had fled her brothers because they had been overprotective. He knew he would have to be subtle if he were going to get her to rest. Like the picnic today. He was sure she had no idea she was being manipulated for her own good.

When Tate awoke, she stretched languorously, unaware that she had an appreciative audience. When she blinked open her eyes she realized it was nearly dusk. She sat up abruptly and made herself dizzy.

Adam was beside her instantly, his arm around her shoulder to support her. "Are you all right?"

"Just a little woozy. I guess I sat up too quickly. Why did you let me sleep so long?"

"You were tired."

Tate leaned her head on his shoulder. "I guess I was. Hadn't we better head back now?"

He nuzzled her neck, searching out the mole near her ear. "I don't have anything planned for this evening. Do you?"

Tate chuckled. "No, I can't say that I have."

Adam slowly laid her back down and found her mouth with his. He brushed his cheek against her long lashes and slid his hands into her hair, smoothing it back where the breeze had ruffled it into her face.

As the sun slipped from the sky, Adam made sweet love to his wife. They rode home by moonlight, and after they had taken care of the horses, Adam made sure Tate went right to bed. In his room. With his arms around her.

"I'll have Maria move your things to my room," he murmured in her ear. "It'll be more convenient since you'll be sleeping in here."

Tate opened her mouth to object and shut it again. After all, she wanted this marriage to work. It made sense that the more time she spent with Adam, the better chance she had of making that happen. She intended to become absolutely irreplaceable in his life.

But as the days turned into weeks, and the weeks into months, the invisible wall of mistrust between them did not come down. Though she made love with Adam each evening, the words "I love you" stuck in Tate's throat whenever she tried to say them. It was too painful to expose her need to him. Especially since she didn't want to put him in the position of feeling he had to say the words back. Which she was afraid he wouldn't.

Adam was equally aware of how much he had gained when he had moved Tate into his bedroom, and how little things had really changed between them. He found himself enchanted by her constant delight in the baby. He tried to be happy with each stage of her pregnancy. Mostly he was successful.

But he watched her and wondered if she ever thought of Buck. The cowboy hadn't been spending much of his free time around the ranch lately. But Adam was watching. Which meant that he still didn't trust her not to seek Buck out if she got the chance.

Meanwhile, he had waited for Tate to tell him again that she loved him. She hadn't said the words lately. Not once, in fact, since they had gotten married. And he found he wanted—needed—to hear those words.

Tate was in bed with Adam when she felt the baby move

for the first time. She grabbed his hand and placed it on her belly. "Can you feel that? Kind of a fluttery feeling."

"No." He tried to remove his hand.

"Wait. Maybe it'll happen again."

"Feel here," Adam said, putting her hand on his arousal. "I think I've got a little fluttery feeling of my own."

Tate couldn't help giggling as Adam's body pulsed beneath her hand. "You've got a one track mind, Dr. Philips."

"Oh, but what a lovely track it is," he murmured, kissing his way down her body. His head lay against her belly when he felt a slight movement against his cheek. He came up off her like a scalded cat.

"I felt it! I felt the baby move!"

Tate smiled triumphantly. "I told you so!"

Adam found himself suddenly uncomfortable. As a doctor he had described the stages of pregnancy to his patients hundreds of times. Yet he found himself overwhelmed by the reality of it. That feather-light touch against his cheek had been an actual human being. Growing inside Tate. A baby that would have his name. A baby that Tate planned to take away with her when she divorced him.

Adam was reminded why he shouldn't let himself care too much about either Tate or the baby. It was going to be bad enough when Tate left him. He wouldn't be able to bear it if he got attached to the child, as well.

Adam didn't say anything about what he was thinking, but from that night onward Tate noticed a distinct difference in his behavior whenever she mentioned the baby. Adam seemed indifferent. Nothing she said got him excited or brought a smile to his face. It was as if the baby had become a burden too heavy for him to bear.

Tate had conveniently forgotten that she had promised Adam a divorce as soon as the baby was born. So she was certain the only possible explanation why Adam wasn't allowing himself to get involved with anything having to do with the baby was because he believed it wasn't his child. She decided to try, once more, to convince him that he was the baby's father.

She chose her moment well. She and Adam had just made love and were lying with their bodies still tangled together. Their breathing had eased and Adam's nose was nuzzled against her throat. The baby was active now, and she pressed her belly against his, knowing Adam couldn't help but feel the movement.

"Adam?"

"Hmm."

"The baby's kicking a lot tonight."

"Hmm."

She threaded her fingers through Adam's hair. "You know, I think he's going to be a lot like his father."

She felt Adam stiffen.

"Like you, Adam. He's going to be a lot like you."

Adam's voice was weary as he said, "You don't have to do this Tate. It's not necessary to try and make me believe the baby's mine. I—" *I'll love it anyway.* Adam bit his lip on that admission. No sense revealing the pain she would be causing him when she took the child away.

"But the baby *is* yours, Adam."

"Tate, we've been through this before. I took tests—"

"What about your wife? Did she take tests, too? Maybe it was her fault and not yours."

"Anne was tested. There was nothing wrong with her."

"Maybe they got your test results mixed up with someone else's," Tate persisted. "I mean, you're a doctor. You know those things happen. Did you see the results yourself?"

"Anne called me from the doctor's office," Adam said.

"You mean you weren't there?"

"I had a medical emergency. I—"

"Then she could have lied!" Tate said.

"Why? She wanted children as much as I did. What earthly reason would she have had to lie?"

"I don't know," Tate said. "All I do know is that a child is growing in my body, and the only man who's put his seed inside me is you!"

For an instant Adam felt a wild surge of hope. Maybe there had been some mistake. Maybe Anne had not lied, but been mistaken. He couldn't believe she would have lied about a thing like that. He had seen her tests himself. The problem did not lie with Anne. So something must have been wrong with him for them to remain childless for eight years.

He felt the hope die as painfully as it had been born. "You're making wishes that can't come true, Tate," he said. "This child isn't mine. I'm sterile."

Tate could have screamed, she was so frustrated. "Is that why you refuse to get involved with anything having to do with the baby?" she demanded. "Because you think it isn't yours?"

"Have you forgotten that you promised me a divorce as soon as it's born?" Adam reminded her.

"What if I said I didn't want a divorce? Would you feel differently about the baby then?" Tate persisted.

"What do you want me to say, Tate? That I'll be a father to

your child? I will. What more do you want from me?" The words seemed torn from someplace deep inside him.

Tate felt frozen inside. It was clear Adam wouldn't ever be able to accept the baby she carried as his own. And she wouldn't subject her child to a lifetime of rejection by its father, the one person who should love and protect it above all others. That knowledge, on top of her doubts about whether Adam loved her, made it plain that she would be better off away from here.

She didn't say another word, just allowed Adam to pull her into his embrace and hold her one last time. Once he was asleep, she carefully disentangled herself. She turned and looked at him once before she left the room—and his life—forever.

 Chapter 11

Garth and Faron were shocked—to put it mildly—when Tate showed up on the doorstep at Hawk's Way.

"What happened?" Garth demanded. "What did that bastard do to you?"

"You look awful, Tate," Faron said, putting an arm around her shoulder and leading her inside.

"If that man hurt you I'll—"

"Don't, Garth!" Tate pleaded. "Just leave it alone. Adam and I are both better off this way."

"Do you want to talk about it?" Faron asked.

"I just want to go to bed and sleep for a week," Tate said.

Faron and Garth exchanged a sober look. There were deep shadows under Tate's eyes. Her face looked gaunt and unhappy.

"He'll pay for the way he's treated you," Garth said.

"No! Listen to me!" Tate said, her voice sharp with fatigue and anxiety. "You have to trust me to know what's best." There it was again. That word *trust*. "This marriage was a horrible mistake. I'm going to file for a divorce."

"Don't be hasty," Faron urged.

"You're dead on your feet. You have no idea what you're saying," Garth countered.

"Stop it! Both of you! *I'm a grown woman.*" She laughed hysterically. "Don't you see? I'm going to be a mother myself! Surely it's time for you to admit that I can manage my own life. You have to love me enough to let go."

Tate didn't wait to hear whether they were willing to concede to her wishes. She was too distressed to deal with them anymore. She ran up the stairs to her bedroom, her rigid bearing defying either one of her brothers to come after her.

"She's changed," Faron said.

"And not for the better," Garth noted.

Faron frowned. "I'm not so sure about that. She's grown up, Garth. She's not a little girl anymore. Six months ago she wouldn't have stood up to you like that. I think she had to be in a lot of pain to leave here in the first place, and a helluva lot more pain to come back. I think maybe we're at least partly responsible."

"I blame the bastard who got her pregnant," Garth said.

"None of this would have happened if she hadn't run away from home. And she wouldn't have run away from home if we hadn't kept such a tight rein on her."

"It was for her own good."

"It doesn't seem that way now, does it?" Faron asked. "I think maybe our little sister grew up in spite of us. And I, for one, am not going to interfere anymore in her life."

ADAM HAD BEEN SCOWLING ever since he had woken up to find Tate gone from his bed—and his life. The first thing he had done was to go hunting Buck. His fury had been boundless when the lanky cowboy was nowhere to be found. Finally, one of the other hands told him Buck had been spending nights with his ex-wife.

That news had confounded Adam. He had doggedly made the trip to Velma's house and knocked on the door in the early hours of the morning. Buck had answered the door wearing low-slung jeans and scratching a head of auburn hair that stood out in all directions.

"Adam! What are you doing here this hour of the morning?"

"Where's Tate?"

"How the hell should I know?" Buck retorted.

By now Velma had joined him, wearing a flashy silk robe, and with her red tresses equally tangled. "What's going on, Adam?"

It was obvious to Adam that Tate wasn't here. But he didn't know where else to look. "Do you mind if I come in?"

"Come on in and I'll make us some coffee," Velma said. "You can tell us what's got you running around at this hour like a chicken with its head cut off."

While Velma was in the kitchen making coffee, Adam put his elbows on the table and wearily rubbed his forehead. Buck waited patiently for Adam to speak his piece.

"Tate's gone. Run away," Adam said at last.

Buck whistled his surprise. "Thought that little filly loved you too much ever to leave you."

Adam's head came up out of his hands. "What?"

"Sure. You and that baby of yours was all she ever talked about."

"*My* baby?"

"Sure as hell wasn't mine!" Buck said.

Adam's eyes narrowed. "She spent nearly the whole night with you. Twice."

Buck laughed in Adam's face. "We were here at Velma's house the first night. And we fell asleep on the banks of the Frio after Velma and I had an argument on the second. There's only been one woman for me. And that's my wife."

"You mean your ex-wife."

Buck grinned and held up his left hand, which bore a gold wedding band. "I mean my wife. Velma and I got married again last Sunday."

"Congratulations. I guess." Adam was confused. "But if you're not the father of Tate's baby, then who is?"

Buck pursed his lips and shook his head. "I would think that has to be pretty obvious even to a blind man."

"But I—" Adam swallowed and admitted, "I can't father children."

"Whoever told you that," Buck said, "is a whopping liar."

"But—" Adam shut his mouth over the protest he had been about to make. Was it really possible? Could Anne have lied to him? It was the only answer that would explain everything.

Adam jumped up from his chair just as Velma brought in the coffeepot.

"You're not staying?" she asked.

"I've got to get in touch with someone in San Antonio." He was going to see the doctor who had done those fertility tests and find out the truth for himself.

"When you're ready to go after Tate, I have a suggestion where you might look," Buck said.

"Where?"

"I figure she went home to her brothers. You'll probably find her at Hawk's Way."

"Damn."

Buck laughed. "I'd like to be a fly on the wall when you try to take her out of there."

Adam wasn't able to think that far ahead. Right now he had a doctor to visit in San Antonio.

Early the next afternoon Adam came out of a glass-walled office building feeling like a man who had been poleaxed.

"Your sperm count was low," the doctor had said. "But certainly still within the range that would allow you to father children."

"But why didn't Anne and I ever conceive children?" he had demanded.

The doctor had shrugged. "It was just one of those things that happens with some couples."

Anne had lied to him. Whatever her reasons—maybe she just hadn't wanted to keep on trying—she had lied to him.

I'm going to be a father! Tate is pregnant with my child!

The realization was only just hitting him. Adam was floating on air. He had always intended to love the child because it was Tate's, but the knowledge that the baby Tate was carrying was a part of him filled his cup to overflowing.

There was only one problem. Tate was at Hawk's Way. And he was going to have to fight her brothers to get her back.

An hour later, he was in his pickup traveling north.

Adam shouldn't have been surprised when he discovered the vastness of Hawk's Way, but he was. The cliffs and canyons in northwest Texas were a startling contrast to the rolling prairies found on the Lazy S.

The ranch house was an imposing two-story white frame structure that looked a lot like an antebellum mansion with its four, twenty-foot-high fluted columns across the front and its railed first- and second-story porches. The road leading to the house was lined with magnolias, but the house itself was shaded by the branches of a moss-laden live oak.

Adam was glad to see that the barn and outbuildings were a good distance from the house. He was hoping to catch Tate alone and talk with her before he had to confront her brothers. He went around to the kitchen door, knocked softly and let himself inside.

Tate was standing at the sink peeling potatoes. She was wearing an apron, and sweat from the heat of the kitchen made her hair curl damply at her nape.

"Hello, Tate."

Tate dropped both potato and peeler in the sink and turned to face Adam. Once she had wiped her hands dry, she kept them hidden in the folds of the apron so Adam wouldn't see how much they were trembling.

"Hello, Adam," she said at last. "I was just peeling potatoes for tonight's pot roast."

"You look tired," he said.

"I haven't been sleeping much the last couple of days." She swallowed over the ache in her throat and asked, "What are you doing here, Adam?"

"I've come to get you. Go upstairs and pack your things. I'm taking you home with me."

"I am home."

"Like hell you are! This is where you grew up, Tate. It isn't your home. Your home is with me and our child."

Tate felt her heart racing with excitement and with hope. Adam's words now were a far cry from what she had heard a mere forty-eight hours ago. It appeared he intended to be a father to the baby after all.

Before Adam could say more, the kitchen door opened and Tate remembered she had told her brothers to come to the house early for lunch because she wanted to take a long afternoon nap. She quailed at the confrontation she knew was coming.

"What the hell are you doing here?" Garth demanded.

"I've come for my wife."

"Tate's not going anywhere," Garth said.

Adam wasn't about to be said nay. He grabbed Tate by the wrist. "Forget your things," he said. "We can get them later." He dragged her two steps, but could go no farther.

Faron and Garth were blocking the way out.

"Get out of my way," Adam said.

"Look, Adam," Faron began in a reasonable voice. "If you'll just—"

But Adam was in no mood to be reasonable. He twisted around to shove Tate out of the way, then reversed the arc with his fist. Faron was felled by the powerful blow, which caught him completely unprepared to defend himself.

Adam stood spread-legged, facing Tate's eldest brother. "I'm telling you to get out of my way."

"You're welcome to leave," Garth said. "But Tate stays here."

"I'm taking her with me."

"That remains to be seen."

Tate knew her brother's strength. He had at least three inches of height and thirty more pounds of muscle than Adam. "Garth, please don't—"

"Shut up, Tate," Adam ordered. "I can handle this on my

own." He was fighting for his life—the right to cherish his wife and raise his child—and he had no intention of losing.

The fight that followed was vicious, but mercifully short. When it was finished, Adam was still standing, but it was a near thing. He grabbed Tate's wrist and helped her step over Garth's body on the way out, letting the screen door slam behind her.

Once Tate and Adam were gone, the two brothers, still sprawled on the floor where Adam had left them, had trouble meeting each other's eyes. Two against one and they were the ones dusting themselves off.

Garth cradled his ribs as he sat up and leaned back against the kitchen cupboards. He pulled his shirttail out and pressed the cloth against a cut over his cheekbone.

Faron stretched his legs out in front of him as he leaned back against the refrigerator. He rubbed his sore chin, then opened his mouth and moved his jaw around to make sure no bones were broken.

"Guess our little sister is married to a man who loves her after all," Faron said.

"One with a damned fine right hook," Garth agreed, dabbing gently with his shirttail at the bruised skin around his eye.

The two brothers looked at each other and grinned. Garth yelped when his split lip protested.

"Guess that's one suitor you couldn't scare off," Faron said.

"I always said Tate would know the right man when he came along."

"Seems you were the one needed convincing," Faron said, eyeing Garth's battered face.

Garth guffawed, then moaned when his head protested. "By

the way, who do you think's going to be godfather to that baby of hers?"

"Me," Faron said, hauling himself off the floor. "You get to be godfather to Jesse's firstborn."

"Jesse's next oldest. It ought to be him."

"Jesse and Adam don't get along. I'm a better choice," Faron said.

The two brothers headed out to the barn, arguing all the way. Neither of them mentioned the fact that they had been relegated to a new role in Tate's life. Their little sister had found a new protector.

Meanwhile, Tate was aware of every move Adam made, every word he spoke. She had him stop at the first gas station they came to with the excuse she had to use the bathroom. She used the opportunity to clean the blood off his face and bought some bandages in the convenience store to put across the cuts on his cheek and chin.

Once they were back in the car, she said, "You were wonderful, you know. I don't think anybody's ever beaten my brother Garth in a fight."

"I had more at stake than he did," Adam mumbled through his split lips.

Tate's spirits soared at this further evidence that Adam's attitude toward both her and the baby had somehow changed.

It was a long ride back home to the Lazy S, broken frequently by stops to allow Tate to use rest room facilities.

"It's the baby," she explained.

"I know about these things," Adam replied with an understanding smile. "I'm a doctor, remember?"

It was dark by the time they arrived back at the Lazy S. Maria greeted them both at the door with a big hug.

"It is so good to see you back where you belong, *señora!*"

In Spanish she said to Adam, "I see you have put the smile back on her face. You will tell her now you love her, yes?"

"When the time is right," Adam said.

Maria frowned. "The time, she is *right now.*"

Adam refused to be pressed. He excused himself and ushered Tate to his bedroom. He lifted her into his arms and carried her across the threshold.

"Our marriage begins now," he said, looking into her eyes. "The past is past."

Tate could hardly believe this was happening. "I love you, Adam."

She waited for the words she knew he would say back to her. But they didn't come.

There was nothing very difficult about saying those three little words, but Adam felt too vulnerable at the moment to admit the depth of his feelings for Tate. He hadn't really given her a choice about coming back with him. It seemed more appropriate to *show* her that he loved her, rather than to tell her so in words.

He made love to her as though she were the most precious being in the world. He kissed her gently, indifferent to his split lip, tasting her as though he had never done so before, teasing her with his teeth and tongue. Her soft whimper of pleasure rolled through him, tightening his body with need.

His hand slid down to her rounded belly. "My child," he whispered in her ear. "Our child."

"Yes. Yes, our child," Tate agreed, glad that he was ready to accept the baby as his own.

"I mean, I know it's mine," Adam said.

Tate was jerked abruptly from her euphoria. "What?" She turned to face him, her eyes still wide and dilated with pleasure. "What did you say?"

Adam's thumb caressed her belly as his eyes met hers. "I went back to that doctor in San Antonio. The one who did the fertility tests on Anne and me. I'm not sterile, Tate. Anne lied to me."

Tate's eyes widened in horror as she realized what this meant. No wonder Adam hadn't said he loved her. He hadn't come to Hawk's Way for her at all. He hadn't fought Garth for the purpose of getting her back. He had fought to get back his child!

Chapter 12

Tate had seized eagerly on her pregnancy as an excuse not
to make love to Adam, and the damned man fell all over himself being understanding. Naturally he wanted to make sure she
took good care of herself so *his child* would be born healthy!

But the next morning, when Adam stood blocking her way
into the office—because she shouldn't have to work in her del-
icate condition—Tate let him have it with both barrels.

"I'm just as capable of working with *your* child growing inside me as I was when it was just *my* child!" she snapped.

"But—"

"No buts! I'll eat right, get enough rest and come through
this pregnancy with flying colors. Even if it is partly *your* child
growing inside me and not just *mine*."

Adam wasn't sure what he had done wrong, but Tate obviously had a bee in her bonnet about something. "What's all this
your child and *my* child business? What happened to *our* child?"

"That was before you found out you can father as many children as you want. Well, you can go father some other fool
woman's kids. This baby's *mine!*"

With that, she shoved him out of the office and slammed the door in his face.

Adam could hear her crying on the other side of the door. He tried the handle and found it was locked. He pounded on the door. "Tate, let me in!"

"I don't want to talk to you. Go away!"

He pounded on the door again. "If you don't open this door, I'm going to break it down," he threatened.

He had just turned his shoulder toward the door when it opened, and he nearly fell inside. "That's better," he said, walking in and shutting the door behind him. "I think maybe we better talk about this…difference of opinion. What's important—"

"I'm not a baby that needs coddling. I'm fully capable of taking care of myself. You have to trust me to—oh, what's the use?" she said, throwing up her hands in disgust. "Trust was never a part of our relationship in the past. I don't suppose that just because you've found out I didn't lie to you about the baby, it's going to change anything between us."

"What does trust have to do with this?"

"Everything!" Tate was quivering she was so upset. "Buck and Velma—"

"Whoa there! What do Buck and Velma have to do with this?" Adam was getting more confused by the minute.

"It doesn't matter," Tate said.

Adam grabbed her by the shoulders. "It obviously *does* matter. Now I want an explanation and I want it now!"

"You sure about that? Food for thought gives some folks indigestion!"

Adam shoved Tate down in the swivel chair and settled his

hip on the desk in front of her. "Settle down now. This kind of agitation isn't good for the baby. I—"

Tate leaped out of the chair and poked a finger at Adam's chest. *"The baby! The baby!"* she mimicked back at him. "That's all you really care about, isn't it? I'm nothing more than a vessel for your seed. I could be a test tube for all the difference it would make to you! Well, I've got news for you, *buster!* I want more than a father for my child, I want a husband to love me and hold me and—" Tate choked back a sob.

"Tate, I do love—"

"Don't say it! If you really loved me, you've had plenty of opportunities to say so. If you say it now I'll know you're just doing it to calm me down for the sake of the baby."

"I'm telling the truth!"

"So was I! When I told you months ago that this baby was yours and mine—*ours!* But you didn't trust me then. And I don't believe you now! Just like Buck and Velma—"

"Are we back to them again?"

"Yes-s-s!" she hissed. "Because Buck and Velma are a perfect example of what happens when there's no trust in a relationship. You hurt each other, and you're miserable and unhappy together.

"If you love somebody you have to be willing to trust them enough to be honest with them. To lay yourself open to the pain of rejection by admitting how you really feel about them. And you have to trust in their love enough to know that they would never do anything purposely to hurt you. Like lying to you. Or sleeping with another man.

"Without trust, love will just wither and die." Tate swallowed another sob and said, "Like it did with Buck and Velma."

"Are you finished?" Adam asked.

Tate sniffled and wiped her nose with the hem of her T-shirt. "I'm finished."

"First of all, I think you should know that Buck and Velma got remarried on Sunday."

Tate's eyes went wide. "They did?"

"Second of all, whether you believe me or not, I do love you. I've loved you for a long time. I never said anything because…"

"Because you didn't trust me," Tate finished in a small voice.

He couldn't deny it, because it was true. "I guess it's my turn to point to Buck and Velma," Adam said ruefully.

"Why?"

"Aren't they proof that people can change? That mistakes aren't irrevocable?"

Tate's brow furrowed. "I suppose."

"Then will you give me a chance to prove how I feel? To prove that I do love you enough to trust you with my heart?"

Tate felt her throat swelling closed with emotion. "I suppose."

"Come here." Adam opened his arms and Tate walked into them. He tipped her chin up and looked deep into her eyes. "We start from here. Our baby, our marriage—"

"Our trust in each other," Tate finished.

They shared a tender kiss to seal the bargain. But it turned into something much more. Or would have, if Maria hadn't interrupted them.

"Señor Adam, there is a man here with the new rodeo bull he says you must sign for."

"I'm coming, Maria."

Adam gave Tate another quick, hard kiss. "Until tonight."

"Until tonight." Tate managed a smile as he turned and left her. He had given her an awful lot to think about. But it was better to confront these issues now, before the baby came, than later. Garth had always said, "If you have a hill to climb, waiting won't make it smaller."

As Adam began to realize over the next several weeks, it was one thing to believe yourself trustworthy; it was quite another thing to earn someone's trust.

He made love to Tate each night, revering her with words and gestures. But he never told her that he loved her. It was plain from the cautious way she watched him when she thought he wasn't looking, that she wasn't yet ready to hear the words—and believe them.

Maria got thoroughly disgusted watching Senor Adam and Señora Tate tiptoe around each other. She nagged at him in Spanish to tell Señora Tate he loved her and be done with it. "If you say it often enough, she will believe it," Maria advised.

"Do you think so?" Adam asked. "Even if she thinks I'm lying through my teeth?"

"But you would not be lying!" Maria protested. "She will see what is in your eyes. And she will believe."

Adam truly wished it were that simple. He was beginning to despair of ever convincing Tate that he loved her enough to want her both as his wife and the mother of his child.

The situation might have gone on unresolved, with both Adam and Tate less than happy, if Maria hadn't decided to take matters into her own hands.

As far as Maria was concerned, it was as plain as white socks on a sorrel horse that Señor Adam loved the little *señora,* and that she loved him. The problem was getting the two of them to recognize what was right in front of their noses.

So right after lunch one day she sent Señor Adam off to

the store to buy some spices she needed for dinner. She waited a half hour, then raced into the office where the *señora* was working.

"Señora Tate, come quick! There's been an accident! Señor Adam—"

By the time Adam's name was out of Maria's mouth, Tate had already left her chair. She grabbed hold of Maria's sleeve and demanded, "How badly is he hurt? What happened? Where is he?"

"It was the new Brahma bull, the one he has penned in the far pasture," Maria said. "He was not watching closely enough and—"

"The bull stomped him? My God! How did you find this out? I never even heard the phone ring! Has somebody called an ambulance? We have to get Adam to a doctor!"

"Señor Buck has already called the doctor. He is with Señor Adam now." Maria smiled inwardly. She hadn't even had to invent an injury for Señor Adam. The *señora* had done that herself. She said, "Señor Buck—"

"Thank God, Buck's with him!" Tate headed for the kitchen to get the keys to her pickup from the peg where she usually left them. But they weren't there.

"Where are my keys? Maria, have you seen my keys?"

Maria closed her hands around the set of keys in her pocket. "No, *señora*. But your horse, she is saddled already for the ride you wished to take this afternoon."

"That'll probably be faster anyway. I can go cross-country. Thanks, Maria. You're a lifesaver!"

Tate had barely been gone ten minutes when Maria heard Señor Adam's pickup pull up in back of the house. She sniffed the onion she had ready and waiting and went running out to

the truck, tears streaming, waving her hands frantically to attract his attention.

"Señor Adam! The *señora!* Hurry!" Maria hid her face in
her apron and pretended to cry.

"What's wrong, Maria? What happened to Tate? Is she all
right?" He didn't wait for an answer, but bounded up the back
steps toward the house.

"She is not there!" Maria cried.

Adam's face bleached white. "She's gone? She left me?"

Maria saw she had made a serious mistake and said, "Oh,
no! But she went riding toward the pasture where you are
keeping that big humped bull. Her horse must have been
frightened. Señor Buck found her there on the ground."

"She's hurt? Has she been taken to the doctor?"

"She is still there. Señor Buck is with her—"

Adam didn't wait to hear more. He jumped back into his
pickup and gunned the motor, heading down the gravel road,
hell-bent-for-leather toward the opposite end of the Lazy S.

Maria dabbed with her apron at the corners of her eyes
where the onion had done its work. Well, she would soon see
the results of her meddling. If she was right, there would be
more smiles and laughter around this house in the future.
When *el bebé* arrived, Tía Maria would tell the story of the
day Papa rescued Mama from the big bad bull and brought her
home to live here happily ever after.

TATE MANAGED TO GET through the gate that led to the new
bull's pasture without dismounting, but she still begrudged the
time it took the mare to respond to her commands as she
opened the metal gate and closed it behind her.

Once she was inside the pasture she kept a sharp lookout for the huge Brahma. She wasn't sure what Buck had done to secure it after it had stomped Adam. The chance that it might still be roaming free in the pasture made her shudder in fear.

Tate hadn't gone far when she heard the sound of a truck spinning gravel somewhere beyond the pasture gate. There was no siren, but she thought it might be the ambulance. Maybe they would know exactly where to find Adam. Tate turned the mare back toward the gate and headed there at a gallop.

She was almost to the gate when she realized the huge Brahma bull, with its thick horns and humped back, was standing there, apparently drawn by the sound of the truck, which usually brought hay and feed.

When the bull heard the horse behind him, he whirled to confront the interloper on his territory. Tate found herself trapped, with no way out. She yanked the mare to a halt, holding her perfectly still, knowing that any movement would make the Brahma charge.

Adam swore loudly and fluently when he realized Tate's predicament. He slammed on the brakes, grabbed a rope from the bed of the truck, and hit the ground running.

"Don't move!" he yelled. "I'm coming."

"Wait!" Tate yelled back. "Don't come in here! It's too dangerous!"

Adam didn't bother with opening the gate, just went over the top and down inside. The rattle of the fence had the bull turning back, certain dinner was about to be served. He stopped, confused when he saw the man on foot inside the fence. He nodded his lowered head from Tate to Adam and back again, uncertain which way he wanted to go.

Adam shook out the lasso and started looking for something he could use as a snubbing post. Not too far away stood a medium-size live oak.

Adam didn't hesitate. He walked slowly toward the Brahma, which began to snort and paw at the ground in agitation. The bull's attention was definitely on Adam now, not Tate.

"Please don't come any closer, Adam," Tate said quietly.

"Don't worry. I've got this all worked out." If he missed his throw, he was going to run like hell and hope he got to the fence before the Brahma got to him.

But Adam's loop sang through the air and landed neatly around the Brahma's horns. He let out the rope as he ran for the live oak. He circled the tree several times, enough to make sure the rope was going to hold when the bull hit the end of it.

By then, Tate had realized what he was doing. She raced her mare to the live oak, took her foot out of the stirrup so Adam could quickly mount behind her, then kicked the mare into a gallop that took them out of harm's way.

The Brahma charged after them, but was brought up short by the rope that held it hog-tied to the tree.

Tate rode the mare back to the gate, where Adam slipped over the horse's rump, and quickly opened the gate for her. Once she was through, he fastened the gate, and reached up to pull her off the mare.

They clutched each other tightly, well aware of the calamity they had barely escaped. As soon as their initial relief was past, they began talking at the same time, amazed by the fact that they had found each other alive and well and unhurt.

"Maria told me the bull had stomped you!"

"She told me you had been thrown from your horse!"

"I wasn't thrown!"

"I wasn't stomped!"

The realization dawned for both at the same time that they had been manipulated into coming here under false pretenses.

"I'll kill her!" Adam said.

"I think you should give her a raise," Tate said with a laugh.

"Why? She nearly got us both killed!"

"Because she made me realize I've been a fool not to believe what I know in my heart is true."

"I do love you, Tate," Adam said. He pulled her into his arms and kissed her hard. "I do love you."

"I know. And I love you. When I thought you might be dying—or dead—I realized just how much."

"When I thought something might have happened to you, I felt the same," Adam said. "I should have been saying 'I love you' every day. I love you, Tate. I love you. I love you."

Adam punctuated each statement with a kiss that was more fervent than the one before.

Tate was having trouble catching her breath. She managed to say, "Adam, we have to do something about that bull."

"Let him find his own heifer," Adam murmured against her throat.

Tate laughed. "We can't just leave him tied up like that."

"I'll send Buck and the boys back to take care of him and to pick up your mare. We have more important things to do this afternoon."

"Like what?"

"Like plotting how we're going to get even with Maria."

As they drove back toward the ranch house, Adam and Tate plotted imaginative punishments they could wreak on the housekeeper for lying to them. It wasn't an easy job, considering how they had to balance her dubious methods against her very satisfying results.

"I think the best thing we could do is have about five children," Adam said.

Tate gulped. "Five?"

"Sure. That'll fix Maria, all right. She'll have the little devils sitting on her lap and tugging at her skirts for a good long while!"

"Serves her right!" Tate agreed with a grin.

Adam stopped the pickup in front of the ranch house, grabbed Tate's hand and went running inside to find the housekeeper.

"Maria!" he shouted. "Where are you?" He headed for the kitchen, dragging Tate along behind him.

"Here's a note on the refrigerator," Tate said.

"What's it say?"

Tate held the note out to Adam.

Dear Señor Adam,
Tell her you love her. I'll be gone for two—no, three—hours.

Love, Maria

Adam laughed and pulled Tate into his embrace—where the first of Maria's little devils promptly kicked his father in the stomach.

THE BLUEST EYES
IN TEXAS

Chapter 1

LINDSEY MAJOR PRESSED her fingers against her temples to ease some of the awful pressure, then rolled onto her side, hoping that would relieve the pain in her head. As she did, her skirt wrapped around her legs. That was odd, because she slept in men's pajamas and had since she was a teenager and thought it was a cool thing to do. She reached a hand down to untangle the yards of material and realized it wasn't just any old skirt, it was ankle-length taffeta. She was still wearing her ballgown!

Lindsey sat up abruptly, which set her head to pounding ferociously and brought a wave of nausea. She fought the sick feeling, sliding her feet onto the floor and carefully pushing herself upright on the edge of the bed. Which was when she realized she wasn't in her own bed upstairs in the Texas governor's mansion. She was…somewhere else.

It wasn't a dream. I was kidnapped right off the front porch of the mansion. I've been drugged. That's why my head hurts.

Lindsey caught a glimpse of herself in the mirror across the room and was appalled at what she found. Her tawny golden hair had fallen from its sleek French twist. The makeup she had sparingly applied to what the press had labeled "the bluest eyes in Texas" was so badly smudged that she looked like a raccoon on a binge. And her beautiful strapless taffeta dress—a glorious shade of lavender that rivaled the remarkable color of her eyes—was crumpled from having been slept in. Lindsey tried to remember what had happened after the struggle on the porch, but drew a blank.

There was no window in the room, no route of escape. She crossed to the only door and slowly, silently, tried the knob. It was locked. She pressed her ear against it, hoping to get some clue as to who had kidnapped her and what terms they were demanding for her release. She could actually make out voices in the next room. Two men were arguing. What they said sent a cold chill down her spine.

"I say we might as well enjoy her while we can. Hector ain't gonna let her go even if the governor commutes the Turk's sentence like he asked and the Turk goes free."

The Turk! Lindsey thought with despair. *I should have known!*

Turk Valerio, the man who had accidentally shot and killed her mother in his abortive assassination attempt on her father five years ago, had been sentenced to die for his crime. The Turk had boasted that he would never be executed, that the Texas Mafia, headed by Hector Martinez, would find a way to set him free. Lindsey had the sinking feeling that she had become a pawn in a very deadly game.

"I want to know what it feels like to do a lady," the man said. "And I sure as hell want to see them blue eyes when I'm pumping into her—before Hector does what he threatened, I mean." The kidnapper made a disgusted sound in his throat. "She's gonna be a mess after that."

"I can see the governor's face when he read that note," a second voice, one with a distinct Texas drawl, said. "'Commute Turk Valerio's sentence by noon tomorrow, or I'm gonna blind the bluest eyes in Texas.' Bet the man turned white as a ghost!" A high-pitched, almost girlish giggle followed.

"Hector won't like it if you touch the girl," a third voice said flatly.

"Well, Hector ain't here," the man with the deep Texas accent retorted. "I agree with Epifanio. I say we enjoy the girl now, while we can. Only, I want her first."

"I get her first, Tex," Epifanio countered. "It was my idea."

"You're too hard on women," Tex complained. "There won't be any left for me."

"I'm telling you both, leave the girl alone," the third voice said.

"Hell, Burr, you wouldn't spoil our fun, would you? Besides, me and Tex together, we're bigger 'n you. I don't think you could stop us all by your lonesome." That horrible, high-pitched laugh resounded again.

"Make a move toward that door and we'll see," the man called Burr replied in a steely voice.

Lindsey's heart was thumping loud and hard in response to the fight-or-flight instinct that had taken over when she realized her peril. They planned to blind her! But they were going to rape her first! Any minute she expected Epifanio and Tex to come bursting through the door—right past the man called Burr, who was all that stood between her and immediate disaster. And good old Burr hadn't said anything about protecting her from the man who wanted to blind her, only from the two men intent on rape.

Lindsey looked around for a weapon. Her eyes alighted on the lamp beside the bed, which had a porcelain base. It ought to make a good club. She quickly pulled the plug from the wall and stripped the lamp of its shade, then dragged a chair over to one side of the door and climbed onto it so the lamp could be wielded from above. She waited, terror stealing her breath and making her suck air in harsh gasps. How much time did she have? How long before she was fighting for her life?

Lindsey watched in breathless horror as the doorknob began to turn.

She brought the lamp down on the head of the first man through the door, who collapsed at her feet with a groan. She stared openmouthed at the second man who filled the doorway. He was huge.

"What the hell?"

She took advantage of the big man's confusion to give him a hard shove. As he fell back through the doorway, she leapt off the chair and darted past him. Unfortunately, he reached out at the last moment and caught her skirt. It tore at the waist but didn't pull free. He began to rein her in like a lassoed heifer.

"You did me a favor, *chiquita,* getting rid of Tex like that. Now I have you all to myself."

Lindsey clawed and kicked, but to no avail. He snagged an arm around her waist and pulled her tight against his chest.

"Let me go!" she cried.

He shook his shaggy-haired head. "Not so fast, *niña.* I like you right where you are."

She kicked him in the shin, which was when it dawned on her she was barefoot. She must have lost her high heels some time during the kidnapping. The blow surely hurt her worse than her assailant, because she yelped in pain, while he just laughed.

She caught sight of the third man—the one who must be Burr—watching her, his fierce, hooded eyes filled with…loathing? She couldn't take her eyes off him, even as Epifanio pulled her body tight against his.

Burr's lips were pressed flat in disgust, distorting the shape of his mouth. His chin had a slight crease down the center of it and jutted as though seeking a confrontation. A diamond sparkled in one earlobe, and she saw a tattoo on his arm below the folded-up sleeve of a black T-shirt, although she couldn't make out what the tattoo was. He had a day's growth of black beard that did nothing to hide the angular planes of his face. His cheekbones were high and wide, and his nose was crooked from having been broken, from the look of it, more than once.

The pull of tearing fabric brought her attention back to the Mexican. She bucked violently to free herself from his grasp.

He ripped the bodice of her gown, exposing the white merry widow beneath it. "Fight me, bitch," he said in a low, rusty-hinge voice. "I like it when a woman fights."

Lindsey didn't disappoint him. Furious and frightened, her fingernails clawed down the side of Epifanio's face, leaving four distinct bloody scratches. She grasped his hair and yanked hard, then reeled when he slapped her across the face with his open hand, drawing blood where her teeth cut her lip.

Lindsey got a quick glance at what appeared to be a coiled black snake tattooed on Burr's arm as he grabbed Epifanio and spun him around. She felt herself pulled free of Epifanio's grasp and flung past him. She hit the wall hard and, momentarily stunned, slid down in a heap.

"I told you to leave her alone."

Dazed, she watched Burr confront Epifanio. He was easily as tall as the Mexican, but lean where the other man was barrel-shaped. His hair was as shiny black as a raven's wing and clubbed into a tail at his nape. He wore tight black jeans and black cowboy boots.

Burr was all sinew and bone. And clearly dangerous. His spread-legged stance was challenging, his balled fists intimidating. A muscle worked where his jaw was clenched. His eyes were a brown so deep it was almost black. There was no compassion in those beautiful dark eyes, just cold-blooded menace.

"Stay out of this, Burr," Epifanio warned. "The woman is mine."

"She belongs to Hector. He'll have your hide if you keep up with what you're doing. Let her be, Epifanio."

Epifanio's eyes narrowed. His lips flattened. "Get outta my way, Burr."

Burr didn't move an inch.

A switchblade appeared in Epifanio's hand. Lindsey flinched when she heard the *snick* as he flipped the blade from its sheath.

"Move outta my way, Burr."

Burr shook his head, a slight, almost imperceptible movement.

Epifanio lunged with the knife, intent on catching Burr by surprise. Burr caught the wrist of the hand that held the switchblade just as it reached his body, turning it aside so the knife skimmed across his chest instead of plunging into it. Lindsey gasped when she saw the streak of red left by the blade.

It dawned on Lindsey that she could escape while the two men were locked in mortal combat. She inched backward toward the door but found it impossible to take her eyes from the drama unfolding before her. It seemed unlikely that Burr would win. He was outmatched in size and strength by the other man. Given that scenario, it was imperative that she escape if she could.

She scrambled toward the door on her hands and knees, forcing herself to ignore the fact that Burr was probably going to die for coming to her rescue. He was a villain, just like the others. If Epifanio didn't kill him, he was going to spend the rest of his life in prison for kidnapping her.

Lindsey pulled herself upright using the doorknob. She had opened the door a mere inch when someone grabbed her, and a flat male palm forced the door shut.

She made a guttural sound deep in her throat that was part outrage, part fear. She turned with her fingers arched into claws aimed at her captor's face, then realized it was Burr who had hold of her. She searched quickly for Epifanio and saw him lying on the floor, the switchblade imbedded in his chest.

Her hand froze in midair, and her stomach revolted at the sight of the dead man. Her eyes shot to Burr's face, which gave no evidence of any feeling whatsoever—neither revulsion nor remorse—for what he had done.

She swallowed back the bile burning her throat. "Is he dead?"

"Yes."

"What are you going to do with me?"

"The hell if I know," he muttered viciously. "We'd damn well better get out of here. Keep your mouth shut when we're in the hall." He opened the door and started to drag her through it.

Lindsey was too terrified to cooperate with her savior—an unshaven man in a black T-shirt and jeans, a man with a pierced ear and a ponytail and a snake tattoo, simply didn't fit her image of a knight in shining armor. "Let me go," she pleaded. "I won't tell them anything about you."

"Look, Blue Eyes—" As Burr spoke, there was a shout from the other room.

It was Tex.

"Hey! Where the hell do you think you're going?" Tex took one look at Epifanio's body, and a gun appeared in his hand from a holster that had apparently been hidden inside his denim jacket. He aimed it in Burr's—and therefore Lindsey's—direction.

"You sonofabitch!" he hissed.

Lindsey squeezed her eyes shut against the sight of the deadly gun bore, waiting for the sound of shots. But there was only one deafening blast, close to her ear. Her eyes flashed open.

Tex lay in the doorway, a pool of blood spreading on the beige carpet around his body.

She turned to stare, horrified, at Burr, who was holding a .38 snub-nosed revolver in his hand. While she watched, he returned the small, deadly weapon to his boot.

Lindsey had been in such a constant state of terror for the past few minutes that her body quivered from excess adrenaline. She felt dizzy, and she wanted desperately to give in to the darkness that threatened to overwhelm her. She wanted even more to live. And she knew that if she fainted now, she might never see daylight again. Her eyes sought out Burr's, wondering what the chances were that he would let her go.

"You're in shock," he said matter-of-factly. He manhandled her over to the couch, forced her to sit, and shoved her head down between her knees. When she tried to rise, he ordered, "Stay there!"

He peered out into the hall, looking to see if anyone was

curious or stupid enough to personally investigate the shot. "We don't have much time. Someone has probably called the authorities about that gunshot."

Lindsey closed her eyes to avoid seeing the two bodies and breathed deeply, trying to regain her equilibrium. She heard Burr pacing the carpet and muttering to himself. He picked up the phone receiver and dropped it back into the cradle.

"Damn! Damn it to hell!"

She sat up and stared at the furious man standing spread-legged across from her with his hands on his hips.

"I guess I don't have any choice," he said. "Come on, let's go."

"Go where?" Lindsey demanded in her most imperious voice.

"Look, Blue Eyes. When I say 'jump' you say 'how high?' Have you got that?" He grabbed a black leather jacket off one of the chairs and slipped his arms into it.

"If you let me go," Lindsey said, "I'll tell my father you saved me from those two men."

"Hell, if I let you go, Hector will just snatch you back up again. Or shoot you or your father or some other member of your family. He means business. You don't have any choice. You're coming with me."

"Where?"

"Damn it, just do what you're told!" He grabbed her arm and yanked her up off the couch.

Lindsey tried to jerk herself free, but ended up nearly wrenching her arm from the socket. She saw the direction

Burr's eyes took as she slammed into him and looked down to see what he found so fascinating. Which was when she realized the extent of the damage to her bodice. The merry widow was far more concealing than many bathing suits she had worn, but it was an undergarment. It did its job well, forcing her generous breasts upward so that a great deal of flesh was mounded above the two white cups.

Burr swore. "You're not going anywhere like that without attracting more attention than I want." He pulled off his jacket and handed it to her. "Put that on."

She looked down the full length taffeta skirt all the way to where her toes curled into the thick carpet. "I don't think your jacket is going to completely solve the problem." It was warm, though, and smelled, surprisingly, of a very male aftershave.

Burr pursed his lips as he observed her bare feet. "I suppose you're right. Guess we'll have to use the stairs down to the garage in the basement."

She started to take the jacket off, and he said curtly, "Keep it."

He didn't give her a chance to protest, just grabbed her hand and headed for the door. He stopped at the portal and turned to her. "If you scream, I'll have to knock you out. Do you understand?"

Lindsey nodded. She had no doubt he would do as he promised. Her mind was racing, trying to think of some way she could escape him. But no one appeared in the stairwell, and she knew he would catch her if she tried to flee. They had nearly reached the garage in the basement. Lindsey knew she

was running out of time. She had to take the chance that someone would hear her and come to her rescue.

She took a deep breath and screamed.

"Damn you, lady! I warned you!"

Lindsey saw the fist coming, felt her teeth snap when flesh
connected with flesh, felt her legs begin to crumple under her.
She was stunned, but not unconscious, so she heard Burr swear
again as he caught her in his arms, threw her over his shoulder in a fireman's carry, and moved stealthily into the garage.

Chapter 2

BURR WAS FURIOUS at the way things had turned out. This wasn't supposed to have happened. He had hoped to let the situation play out naturally. But Tex and Epifanio had gotten the bright idea to rape the governor's daughter. He couldn't let that happen, so he had interfered.

And blown eighteen months of undercover work as a member of the Texas Mafia.

He damned all spoiled little rich girls, like Miss Lindsey Major, who believed they were immune to the rules that applied to everybody else, who considered themselves too far above the vermin that roamed the dark alleys of the world to ever be threatened by them. She had been told that Hector Martinez was planning something. Burr had risked a great deal to make the anonymous phone call to the governor's mansion himself. She had answered the phone, so he knew she had been made aware of the danger. And damned if she hadn't ignored his warning and gone out to that charity ball after all!

She had cavalierly dismissed the security man at the end of the walk, instead of having him escort her to the front door of the mansion—where she had been snatched and dragged back into the concealing forsythia bushes before she could get inside.

But he had to admire her spunk. No tears from Miss Lindsey Major, just clawed fists and fight. Unfortunately, she had complicated things by screaming when he had warned her to be quiet. God only knew what repercussions there would be when word got out that he had hit her.

Hell, he hadn't wanted to take the job in the first place, but the captain of the Rangers had convinced him that someone had to do it. The last Texas Ranger they had sent undercover, Burr's best friend, Lieutenant Larry Williams, had been found dead in his car trunk. Burr was a natural to take Larry's place, the captain had said, because he had grown up in the gangs in Houston along with Larry, and he knew the rackets. He had the snake tattoo from his youth and understood the lingo. A pierced ear and long hair and a black leather jacket had completed his disguise. No one with the Texas Mafia had suspected Burr Covington was actually a lieutenant in the Texas Rangers.

He had been really close to nailing Hector Martinez for the murder of his friend, but all that effort was down the john now. It was some comfort to know he would be able to convict Hector of kidnapping the governor's daughter. But they would have to catch Hector first, and that was going to be more difficult than it sounded. Hector had more underground hiding places than a rattlesnake.

Burr wasn't sure what to do now. He had been hoping against hope that he could continue his role undercover. But after what he had done to Epifanio and Tex, and with the governor's daughter in his custody, there wasn't much chance of that. He needed to get in touch with Captain Rogers and find out what he was supposed to do with the woman. With any luck, it would be a simple matter of tucking her away somewhere safe until they either caught Hector or the Turk's death sentence was carried out.

Burr set the governor's daughter down on the passenger side of a black Jaguar with black leather seats. The car happened to be his own, but it fit the image he had been portraying, so he had used it. He saw the woman was regaining consciousness, so he gave her cheek a little slap.

"Wake up," he said. "We need to talk."

He might as well tell her who he was, Burr figured. That way she was more liable to cooperate. Although, even that wasn't a guarantee. A woman used to ordering people around, a woman used to having her own way, wasn't going to like taking orders. Only, Burr was determined to stay in control of the situation, even if she was the governor's daughter and had the damnedest blue eyes he had ever seen. Not to mention a few other hard-to-ignore assets.

His gaze slid to the opening in his jacket, where her breasts rose as she heaved in a deep breath and let it out in a shuddering sigh. He had an uncontrollable urge—which he carefully controlled—to put his mouth against her flesh to see if it was as delectable as it looked.

He heard her gasp and lifted his gaze to meet hers. Damn, but her eyes were beautiful! They were wide-set and heavily lashed and large enough for a man to get lost in. He could see why they said she had the bluest eyes in Texas. Except, they weren't blue, really. More a sort of lilac color. But definitely unique and absolutely dazzling.

Now he noticed that the rest of her features were rather ordinary. Her nose was small and straight, her mouth wide and full. Her chin jutted slightly, but he figured that was probably because she made a habit of leading with it. She was always going to attract male attention with her lush figure, and her mane of golden hair was indeed a crowning glory.

It was said she used those eyes of hers to put a man on his knees and get her own way. Well, those baby blues weren't going to work on him.

All the same, he felt a jolt of guilty shame when she accused him of wrongdoing with her eyes and followed that with the outraged statement, "You hit me!"

With an effort, he managed a shrug. "It was your own damn fault. I warned you not to scream."

He watched as she pulled the jacket closed. So. She had caught him looking at her. She must be wondering what his intentions were. Hell, he wouldn't mind having her under him in bed. What man wouldn't? But he knew better than to think he could have what he wanted. She was the governor's daughter. He was a man who had grown up on the wrong side of the tracks.

He bent down on one knee beside the open door and realized with an inward sigh that she had brought him to his knees, after all. "Look, Blue Eyes—Miss Major—we have to talk."

She swallowed hard but said nothing.

He was uncomfortable kneeling beside the door, and there was always the chance she would get it into her head to scream again. He stood and closed the car door and started around the front of the Jaguar to the driver's side.

Before he had gotten halfway around the car, she shoved open her door and ran, screaming at the top of her lungs.

Burr caught her before she had gone twenty feet, tackling her like a football player, the two of them rolling over and over until they were stopped by a concrete abutment in a dark corner of the garage. He came to rest lying on top of her, uncomfortably aware of the feminine shape beneath him. His body reacted instantly, instinctively.

Burr was embarrassed and unable to stop the slow flush that climbed his throat. His body had responded like some randy teenager's to the feel of her flesh between his thighs, rather than like the rational, professional, thirty-six-year-old Texas Ranger he was. Hell, he was probably going to have to answer to the captain for that, too.

Lindsey recognized the hardness pressing against her abdomen and felt a renewed terror at her predicament. Worse,

Burr's weight kept her from taking a breath, which she desperately needed since the fall had knocked the wind from her.

She knew frustration when she saw it. Her father rarely lost his temper, though he could become dangerously angry. Burr's dark eyes burned now with that same controlled fury.

"Damn you. I ought to…" He didn't finish his threat. His eyes searched the garage, looking for whoever might have heard her scream.

Her mouth worked as she gasped, "Please… Please. I…can't breathe."

He eased his weight onto his arms, but held her captive with his lower body—his aroused lower body. "That was a stupid thing to do, Blue Eyes."

She noticed he had given up the deferential *Miss Major*.

She felt a surge of hope when she saw a couple come out of the elevator and start toward their car.

"Don't make a sound," Burr hissed in her ear.

Lindsey opened her mouth to scream.

And Burr covered it with his.

There was nothing sensuous about his kiss. It was brutal, intended to keep her silent until the couple was gone. She bucked with all her strength at the same time she tried to bite him.

His mouth flattened, but he didn't otherwise respond to the pain she knew she must be causing him with her teeth. His hips pressed her down, so she felt the roughness of the concrete against her legs and back where her gown was rucked up.

She heard a car starting and the squeal of rubber on cement

as it drove away. She closed her eyes so Burr wouldn't see the defeat she felt. A moment later he caught both her hands in one of his, while his other hand replaced his mouth to silence her.

"Look at me," he demanded. He used his hold on her to force her face toward him when she didn't respond and repeated, "Look at me!"

Lindsey opened her eyes and looked at him defiantly.

"In a moment I'm going to let you go. If you scream, I will knock you out—all the way out. Blink those pretty blue eyes of yours if you understand."

She blinked her eyes once, slowly.

He removed his hand, then stared at her, daring her to scream.

Burr watched in consternation as tears welled in the bluest eyes in Texas. They made her eyes luminescent and, he decided, even more attractive. He was aroused again—or still. And she was obviously terrified of him because of it. He quickly levered himself off her and reached down to help her up. She refused his hand, stumbling to her feet.

Burr was just about to start explaining things when she ran again. He quickly caught her, shoving her up against the concrete wall. He stapled her hands flat on either side of her head against the rough surface and snapped, "Damn it, I'm a Texas Ranger! I've been working undercover. You're safe. Do you hear me? You're safe!"

"A Texas Ranger?"

Burr nodded curtly.

He felt her whole body relax against him. Then the tears

came in earnest. It was obvious she was fighting them, and he debated whether he ought to try to comfort her. But that sort of thing could be easily misconstrued, and he already had enough to answer to the captain for.

The heartrending sound of a broken sob moved him to put his arms around her and, once he had done that, it seemed the most natural thing in the world to pull her into his embrace and murmur calming words in her ear. His body once again reacted in a totally male way to her femaleness.

Burr had never had much use for prima donnas, and Lindsey Major certainly qualified as one. Unfortunately his body didn't know a thing about her personality; it was reacting strictly to the primeval need of male for female. He tightened his hold, feeling the swell of her breasts against his muscular chest.

Lindsey had thrown her arms around the Texas Ranger in relief, and they caught in the ponytail at his nape, which was surprisingly silky. She trembled at the feel of Burr's lips, soft and soothing against her forehead as he crooned words of comfort. And she was aware, again, of the fact that he was attracted to her in a way that was totally inappropriate to the situation.

Now that she was no longer in terror for her life, however, she realized with no little distress that his arousal had sparked an answering response from her. It was easiest to attribute her reaction to the Ranger as simple relief that he wasn't one of the bad guys. It couldn't possibly be more than that. She didn't know this man and, judging from the looks of him, he wasn't someone she would ever want to know. It would be best to defuse the situation as quickly as possible.

"You can let me go now," she said.

"What?" Burr had been so caught up in the pleasure of what he was doing that he was slow to notice the governor's daughter withdrawing from his embrace.

He met her gaze and saw the tears were gone, replaced by an icy look of disdain. The governor's daughter—a woman the newspapers had recently labeled an elusive ice princess because she was never seen twice with the same male escort—was back.

Burr stepped away, grabbed Lindsey's arm and, without looking back, dragged her toward his car.

Naturally she resisted. "Where are you taking me?"

Burr raised a brow at her commanding tone of voice. "Somewhere you'll be safe."

"I demand that you take me home."

"I'm afraid that isn't possible right now."

She dug in her heels, and he was forced to stop or hurt her. He didn't want to be accused of using unnecessary force.

"I insist you let me call my father right now and tell him I'm all right."

"Not here." Anticipating her argument, he explained, "There's still a chance one of Hector's goons may show up."

She hesitated, evaluating what he had said. "All right, I'll go with you. But we stop as soon as it's safe, and I call my father. Agreed?"

"Agreed." Of course, her idea of when it might be safe to stop and his probably differed. But Burr didn't think this was the time to bring that up.

The Jaguar was the kind of car Lindsey expected a man like Burr to own. Racy. Fast. Dark. Dangerous. She wondered if he had been given the car as part of his cover and realized she was having trouble making the leap from "bad guy" to "good guy" where he was concerned. Burr simply didn't look the part of guardian angel.

Burr opened the passenger door, shoved Lindsey in less carefully this time, and slammed it behind her. He slid over the hood and got in on the other side. The engine started with a roar that became a purr as he pulled out of the garage. He slipped from the city street onto I-35 and accelerated.

Lindsey blinked her eyes against the bright sunlight. The instant she realized Burr had gotten onto the interstate, her alarm returned. "Where are you going?"

"I told you, somewhere Hector can't find you."

Her eyes widened. "You never intended to let me make a phone call, did you?" She reached for the door handle.

"Don't even think about jumping out," he said. "You'd end up seriously injured or dead. Trust me."

"*Trust* you? First you hit me, then you fall on me like a beast in rut and manhandle me like I was some criminal, and now you're driving me God knows where and threatening me with dire consequences if I try to leave your august presence! Give me one good reason why I should trust you."

"I saved your life."

There was a moment of silence. "Well, there is that," she conceded ruefully.

"Look, I can't take you anywhere near the governor's mansion until I talk to my captain. Hector may have someone watching the place. I don't want to be seen returning you home. In fact, I've got to find someplace to hide us both."

"Why do you have to hide?" Her eyes went wide with a sudden horrible thought. "You weren't lying about being a Ranger, were you?"

His lips curled in a bitter smile. "No, I'm a Ranger, all right. But there's a slight problem nobody counted on."

"What's that?"

"Hector is liable to be a bit perturbed when he finds out I killed his brother."

"His brother?"

"Epifanio."

"Oh, no!"

Lindsey bit her lip worriedly as Burr exited west onto U.S. 290 heading toward Fredericksburg and the hill country. A long, poignant silence developed as she watched the miles fly by. Her glance slid to the man driving the Jaguar. Maybe she simply hadn't given him the right incentive to take her home.

"I'm sure my father would reward you generously—with a great deal of money—if you would just take me home."

"Do you think you're worth it?"

She arched an aristocratic brow. "What do you mean?"

"I know for a fact you were warned not to go out last night. Why did you?"

"That's none of your business."

"You made it my business when you got yourself kidnapped."

"I had promised to attend the ball. I had to go."

"So you were just doing what spoiled little rich girls do, is that it?"

"Spoiled—" Lindsey bit back her retort. She wasn't going to argue with a man wearing a ponytail and a diamond earring. "You know nothing about me."

"I know what I read in the papers."

Lindsey laughed. "I suspected you were a fool. Now I've got proof."

He glanced sharply at her.

"Anyone who believes what he reads in the papers—"

"Is a fool?" he interrupted. "But then, I've had a chance to judge you for myself now. At least one thing they said is true. You've got the bluest eyes I've ever seen. And from the looks of you, I'm inclined to believe there's some truth in the rest of what I've read."

"You mean, that I'm spoiled rotten, the 'very much indulged' daughter of a very powerful man?" Lindsey said, her voice rife with indignation as she quoted a recent society news article.

"If the panty hose fit…"

He took his eyes off the road long enough to give her a thorough perusal with eyes that held their share of disapproval and disdain.

Lindsey gave him a withering look of scorn. "Appearances can be deceiving."

He snorted. "You can say that again."

She noticed with some alarm that he had turned off the highway onto a winding dirt road that was shaded by live oaks. "Where are we going?"

"Someplace private where I can use the phone."

"Remember, I want to talk to my father."

He brought the Jaguar to a stop in front of a small wooden cabin with a roofed porch and a stone chimney. The cabin was unpainted, and the split wood had been aged by wind and weather. There was a picture window in front, with a door to one side of it.

"Get inside," he said.

Lindsey sat where she was.

"Go on," he said. "There's no one here but us."

Lindsey stayed where she was. "What is this place?"

Burr exited the car, slid over the hood and opened her door. "Are you coming out of there on your own, or am I going to have to drag you out?"

Lindsey dipped a bare foot out of the car. She winced when she encountered the small, sharp stones on the drive. Before she had taken two painful steps, Burr swept her up into his arms. She instinctively grabbed his shoulders. The muscles beneath the T-shirt were rock hard. Her eyes met his, questioning.

"You don't weigh as much as I thought you would."

She flushed at the insult buried in the compliment. She was

five-ten in her stocking feet, and nobody had ever accused her of being skinny. Fortunately, he was easily six inches taller. He carried her up to the porch and set her down.

She didn't thank him. After all, it wasn't her fault she didn't have any shoes.

Burr opened the door and gave her a nudge inside.

Lindsey lifted her chin and, once she regained her balance, walked past him as regally as a queen. She thought she heard him grunt in disgust, but refused to give him the satisfaction of a response.

She looked around the cabin, which was sparingly furnished. There was an old leather couch and a rawhide-covered chair in front of the stone fireplace. The hardwood floor was polished to a high sheen, but there were no rugs of any kind on it. Nor were there curtains on any of the windows.

She could see the kitchen from the living room. It contained a small wooden table and two ladderback chairs. She suspected the other doorway led to the bedroom and bath. There wasn't room for much else.

She turned to face Burr with her hands folded in front of her. "Now what?"

"Now I have to make some calls."

Lindsey looked around for a phone, but didn't see one.

"Not here," he said. "I have to go into town."

"What am I supposed to do while you're gone?"

"Wait here for me."

Lindsey swallowed her outrage and managed to say in a reasonable voice, "Why can't I go with you?"

"I can't take the chance you'll draw attention with those blue eyes of yours. You'll be safer here."

"I can always wear sunglasses," she snapped.

"I don't have a pair handy. Do you?"

Obviously she didn't.

"You'll be safer here," he said.

"Safer?" she asked in a sharp voice. "What if one of Hector's men finds me here? I'm totally defenseless!"

Burr snorted. "I wouldn't say that. You didn't do so badly at the hotel."

"You know what I mean," she said with asperity. "I know what Hector had planned for me. I heard you talking through the door." She paused and admitted, "I'm scared."

Burr's eyes narrowed. He seemed to debate a moment before he spoke. "You've got nothing to fear if you stay here."

Lindsey looked at him, really looked at him. At the long hair. The earring. The twice-broken nose. The snake tattoo. "I repeat, I don't see anything that leads me to believe I can trust you to have my best interests at heart."

"As someone recently told me, appearances can be deceiving."

"I won't stay here alone," she said. "The moment you're gone, I'll walk back to the road."

"I'm sorry to hear that."

He moved amazingly fast, catching her arms and dragging them behind her. He found rope in the kitchen and tied her hands. He wasn't precisely rough, but he yanked the clothes-line cord tight around her wrists. He pushed her toward the open doorway that led to what turned out to be, as she had suspected, the bedroom.

He picked her up and dumped her on the bed before tying her ankles together. "You should do all right here until I come back."

"How long is that going to be?" She felt humiliated and in-dignant, and both of those emotions were apparent in her voice.

"Not long enough for you to work yourself free of those ropes," he said, as though reading her mind. "Just lie still and be good. I'll bring you back something to eat."

Lindsey suddenly realized she was famished. It had been al-most twenty-four hours since her last meal. But she refused to be mollified by the bone he had thrown her. "My father will have your badge when he hears about how you've treated me. You'll be writing parking tickets for the rest of your life!"

"I'm sorry to have to do this," he said as he tied a pillow-case around her mouth. "I don't think there's anybody around to hear you if you scream, but I can't take the chance."

Then he was gone. She heard stones scattering as he left the driveway. She immediately tested her bonds, but they didn't give. She began looking around the room to see what she might use to cut herself free. Then it dawned on her that he hadn't tied her to the bed. There was nothing to keep her from just getting up and hopping away.

BURR WAS WORRIED. He wondered whether it might not have been smarter to take the governor's daughter home, after all.

But he knew that wouldn't have solved anything. Hector would just make some attempt on some other member of the family. No, this had to be solved while Hector still thought someone on his side had the woman.

Burr was also angry with himself for not finding some other way to rescue "the bluest eyes in Texas" without having to kill Hector's brother. But he hadn't been given a choice. At least he had the girl—the woman, he corrected himself—to bargain with. And what a woman!

Lindsey Major was the kind of woman he had always dreamed about, whenever he let himself dream. She was tall, with lush curves and soft skin. He knew about the soft skin because he'd had to touch her to tie her up. And he knew about the curves because he had picked her up and held her in his arms.

Burr felt his body respond to the memory of how she had felt with her warm breasts nestled against his chest. He cursed under his breath. He might as well desire some image on a movie screen. He had about the same chance of intimacy with the governor's blue-eyed daughter.

He found a phone booth in the small town closest to the cabin. The town consisted of a gas station and a general store, which also contained a post office. People stopped here for gas or to get a soda on their way to hunt in the hill country, or on their way to go floating down the many streams in the area on an inflated inner tube. He hadn't come here once in the eighteen months he had worked for Hector, and he was pretty sure there was no way Hector could trace him here.

He called the governor's mansion, knowing that was where the captain would be. It took a while for someone to acknowledge who he was and to get the captain on the phone.

"I've been compromised," Burr said.

"Damn!" A pause and then, "Is she safe?"

"I've got her."

"Where?"

"At my cabin in the hill country."

"What happened?"

"I had to kill Hector's brother."

"Come on in, Burr. The game's up."

Burr shook his head, then realized Captain Rogers couldn't see him. "No, Captain. I haven't spent the past eighteen months undercover with these bastards to have it all go down the drain now. I think I can still get Hector. But I need to do something with the governor's daughter. Is there someplace I can drop her off?"

There was a long pause, and Burr heard Captain Rogers discussing the situation with those around him.

"You there, Burr?"

"Yes, sir."

"I want you to call Hector and tell him you're willing to deal for the governor's daughter." Frank continued speaking, telling Burr the details of the plan he had worked out with the other law enforcement officials who had responded to the governor's call for assistance.

When Frank had finished, Burr said, "I don't like it. I could manage better without the woman."

"She's safe with you. We'll take care of Hector."

"Hector's not going to deal unless he sees me in person," Burr said.

"You call him. Offer him the deal. Then sit tight with Miss Major."

"I think Miss Major would be happier if she went home."

"That's not an option, Burr."

"But, sir—"

"Don't waste your breath arguing. The decision has been made. Miss Major stays with you."

Burr heard someone ask for the phone.

"This is Governor Major. Who am I speaking to?"

"This is Ranger Lieutenant Covington," Burr replied.

"How is my daughter?" the governor asked. "Is she all right?"

Burr heard the emotion in the governor's voice. *He's going to have my head, all right. Just like she said.* "She's fine, Governor."

"She's not hurt?"

"No, sir. She's just as beautiful as the newspapers say. And just as contrary." Burr swore under his breath. *Why did I say that? I'm going to get my tail kicked all the way back to Austin for insubordination.*

He heard the governor chuckle. "That's my girl, all right." He gave a patent sigh of relief. "Thank you, Lieutenant Covington. Take care of her for me."

"Yes, sir. I will, sir."

"You heard the governor, Burr," the captain said. "I'll get

back to you when we've taken care of Hector. Until then, you take care of Miss Major."

"Yes, sir." Burr waited for a click, then slammed the phone onto the hook. A moment later he picked it up again and began to dial.

When Hector came on the line, Burr pricked him by asking, "Did you lose something?"

"Where is she?" Hector demanded.

"I've got her."

"What happened?"

Burr said nothing.

"I asked you what happened."

"They gave me no choice."

"The girl belongs to me. I want her."

"I want to make a deal, Hector."

"You bring her to me now, and I might let you live," Hector said. "Otherwise, I'll hunt you down. And kill you and the girl both."

Burr quickly gave Hector the terms Captain Rogers had outlined. When Hector arrived at the rendezvous site, there would be law enforcement officials of all kinds waiting to apprehend him.

"I'll keep the girl as insurance," Burr said. "You'll get her when you show up with the money."

"You're a dead man, Burr," Hector said.

"If you don't get the girl back, you can't negotiate with the governor for the Turk's life," Burr reminded him.

Burr hung up the phone on Hector's threat to kill him slowly when he caught up to him. After a stop to buy supplies, he was careful not to be seen leaving town and watched to make sure he wasn't being followed when he turned onto the dirt road that led to the cabin.

It was time he had a talk with the governor's daughter. He went directly to the bedroom where he had left her.

She was gone.

Chapter 3

IF SHE HAD POSSESSED a decent pair of shoes, Lindsey thought, she could have made it to the main road. But the men's cowboy boots she had found in the closet of the cabin weren't doing the job, even with two extra pairs of socks.

She hid behind a tree when she saw the Jaguar returning along the dusty road. Burr would know in a moment or two that she was gone, and he would come looking for her. There was no sense running. Not in these damned boots. But she wasn't sure she wanted to give up, either. Being in Burr's custody hadn't exactly been a picnic so far.

She rubbed her shoulder where she had bruised herself falling out of the high, four-poster bed, and ran a gentle finger over the cuts at her wrists where she had used a knife from the kitchen to free herself. It had been stupid to try to escape. In all probability, her father had demanded her return, and Burr had come back to set her free.

She hadn't decided yet whether she was going to complain about what Burr had done to her. He was responsible for more than a few of the bruises she now bore. She moved her jaw cautiously. It was swollen and sore, but she was pretty sure he hadn't hit her as hard as he could have.

"Have a nice walk?"

Lindsey stiffened at the sarcasm in Burr's voice. She turned slowly to face him, gritting her teeth when she saw the amusement in his eyes at the outfit she was wearing.

"You look like a little girl dressed up in her father's clothes."

Lindsey looked down at the oversize orange University of Texas sweatshirt, men's jeans, and boots she was wearing. The jeans were held up with some of the rope that had been used to tie her hands. "This was all I could find."

"If you'd just been a little patient, I would have solved the problem for you. I bought some things for you in town."

"I won't need them, because you're going to be taking me home," Lindsey said in a firm voice.

He shook his head. "I'm afraid not."

"My father—"

"I spoke to the governor personally. He agreed you'd be safer with me until Hector's been picked up."

Lindsey felt her chin begin to tremble. "How long is that going to take?"

"Until tomorrow, if we're lucky."

"And if we're not?"

"We'll worry about that when the time comes." Burr

reached out a hand and traced the bruise on her jaw. "I'm sorry about that."

Lindsey jerked her head away. "You've got a lot more than that to be sorry for!"

His eyes grew cold. "I was doing my job the best way I knew how. If you had paid attention to the warnings you were given—"

"I had no warning about anything like this!"

"You were told Hector was making plans."

Lindsey bit her lip. "I didn't think—"

"Your kind never does," Burr interrupted.

Lindsey's face flamed with anger "This isn't my fault!"

"It sure as hell isn't mine!" Burr retorted. "I spent eighteen long, lousy months undercover with the Texas Mafia, trying to get enough information to prove Hector Martinez ordered the death of a friend of mine. Thanks to you, prosecuting Hector for that crime isn't going to happen now."

There was a pause while Lindsey absorbed what he had said. "I'm sorry."

"Yeah, well, sorry doesn't cut it, Blue Eyes."

"Don't call me that!"

"I have it on good authority—the news media—that you're the lady with the bluest eyes in Texas."

"My eyes have nothing whatsoever to do with who I am."

"What you are is arrogant and uncooperative."

"How dare you—"

"You ready to walk back now?"

Lindsey stuck her chin in the air and began walking back toward the cabin. Her stride was hampered by a broken blister on her left heel.

"Something wrong with your leg?"

Lindsey heard the concern in Burr's voice, but answered haughtily, "Nothing that concerns you."

She continued her determined limp toward the cabin.

Lindsey gave a cry of surprise as Burr swung her up into his arms, shifting her until he was holding her close, with her breasts crushed against his chest. Her arms involuntarily circled his neck. She sought out his face and was surprised to find his eyes hooded, his nostrils flared. She was unnerved by the male energy vibrating from the man whose arms had closed securely around her shoulders and under her knees. Her eyes came to rest on his mouth, which was partly open, the lips full, the mouth wide.

"What do you think…" Her voice was raspy, so she cleared her throat and tried again. "What do you think you're doing, Mr.—? What *is* your last name, anyway?"

"Covington," Burr replied. "I thought I'd give you a lift back to the cabin." He had already started walking, in fact. He kept his eyes focused straight ahead.

"Did it ever occur to you that I would rather walk than be put in the position of accepting your help?"

"There are a lot of things that occur to me when I think about you." *Like how good you feel in my arms. Like how those blue eyes of yours would look if I was inside you making sweet, sweet love to you.*

Lindsey didn't bother asking Burr to explain himself. She didn't want to exacerbate the situation. She held on to his neck because that eased the weight he had to carry in his arms, not because the silky hair at his nape felt good. She snuggled closer so he wouldn't drop her, not because she liked the feel of hard muscle pressing against her breasts. And she laid her face against his throat so she wouldn't have to look at him, not because she wanted to smell the essence of him on his skin and clothes.

When they arrived at the cabin, Burr set her down on the porch and offered her an olive branch. "Look, if we're going to be stuck together for the next twenty-four hours, we may as well call a truce."

"I wasn't aware there was a war going on."

Burr snickered. "Fine, Blue Eyes. I don't mind the sniping if you don't."

"Wait!" Lindsey laid a hand on Burr's arm. She recoiled when she realized she had touched the snake tattoo.

His lips curled in a cynical smile. "Not the kind of thing you're used to, is it?"

Lindsey's eyes narrowed. "I don't understand why you're so determined to insult me. And I should mention, it isn't doing your career any good."

"Is that a threat, *Blue Eyes?*" Burr said in a low voice.

"That would be rather foolish under the circumstances," Lindsey conceded. "I am, after all, at your mercy for the next twenty-four hours. It would seem discretion is the better part of valor. Truce?" She held out her hand for Burr to shake.

Burr's hand enveloped hers, and she realized for the first time how big he was, and how strong, and that his palm and fingertips were calloused as though he worked with his hands. Perhaps he did in his spare time. She knew little or nothing about him.

"You can change in the bedroom while I cook us something to eat."

Lindsey disappeared into the bedroom and shut the door behind her. She was surprised at how well the jeans fit, not to mention the tennis shoes. However, she decided she would rather walk barefoot until she could find a Band-Aid for the blister on her heel. She pulled on a T-shirt that pictured a dead armadillo on the front with the words Road Kill blazoned across it and headed back to the kitchen.

Burr was dismayed at how the jeans fit her. They outlined her legs and fanny too well. And the T-shirt was downright dangerous. She had obviously abandoned the merry widow, and he could see the soft curve of her breasts beneath the cotton. He frowned when he realized she was barefoot. The sight of her toes curling on the hardwood floor made her look as vulnerable as a child. Only she was a full-grown, red-blooded woman. And his body responded to her like a full-grown, red-blooded man.

"The shoes didn't fit?" He was amazed at how rough his voice sounded. He turned back to the stove to hide the bulge that was making his jeans uncomfortably snug.

"I was wondering if you have a Band-Aid."

At his look of confusion, she set her bare foot up on the counter beside him and showed him the blister on her heel.

"See?"

Whoever would have thought an ankle could be such a source of erotic stimulation? Burr stared at her foot until his eyes glazed, then forced his attention back to the potatoes he was frying on the stove. "Don't have a Band-Aid. I'll get one tomorrow when I go into town."

"Guess I'll have to go barefoot until then." She put her foot back on the floor and wiggled her toes. "It feels kind of nice," she admitted. "I can't remember the last time I walked around barefoot. Oh, yes, I do," she said.

To Burr's relief, she wandered to the kitchen table and sat down. He bent over and checked the steaks in the oven broiler to hide his state of arousal.

"I was six, and my mother and father took me to Padre Island, to the beach. My mother was pregnant with Carl—he's my younger brother—and I got to race up and down the beach barefoot. I loved it."

"That was a long time ago," Burr said.

"Yes, it was. Those were some of the last carefree days my family had. Father entered politics that year. I didn't see as much of him after that. He was always on the road campaigning, first for state representative, then for congressman, and finally for governor."

Talk about Lindsey's father reminded Burr of who she was, and why he had to keep his distance. If he was lucky, he would get out of this situation with no more than a reprimand. If he let his libido get out of hand, there was no telling what the consequences would be. Only, it was damned hard to remember who she was when she was slouched back comfortably in the kitchen chair with her fingers meshed behind her head, raising the tips of her breasts against the T-shirt. Her right ankle was crossed over the opposite knee, in a naturally sexy pose.

He checked the steaks again. "These are about ready. How do you like yours?"

"Pink."

The word brought to mind all kinds of things Lieutenant Burr Covington would rather not think about. Lips. Blushing cheeks. Nipples. *Damn it, Covington, get your mind off the woman! She's out of bounds. Got it?*

"Do you have any wine?" she asked.

Burr stared at her in confusion.

"To go with the steak," she explained. "I love a dry red wine with steak."

Burr snorted. "I've got some beer."

"Lite?"

He snorted again, only this time it turned into a rumbly sort of laugh. "Hell, Blue Eyes, how about a diet cola?"

Her eyes reflected her disappointment, but she said, "I'll take it." And then, to explain herself, added, "I never learned to like beer, but the lite beers don't seem to taste as bad."

"You wouldn't have lasted long in my neighborhood," Burr muttered.

"What neighborhood is that?" Lindsey inquired.

"The wrong side of the tracks in Houston."

"Is that where you got the tattoo?"

Burr held his arm up and looked at it as though the tattoo had suddenly appeared there. "Yeah."

"May I look at it?"

He held his arm toward her. To his chagrin, she got up from the table and came over to him. He held his breath as she traced the shape of the coiled, hooded cobra with her fingertips.

Then she looked up at him, catching him like a deer in a set of headlights with those blue eyes of hers. "Does the snake mean something special?"

"It was an initiation rite of the gang I was in as a kid." He rubbed his skin, which was suddenly covered with goose bumps, brushing her hand away in the process.

"You were in a street gang in Houston?" Her eyes went wide with astonishment.

"Yeah."

"What? I mean…how…"

"The steaks are done," Burr said. "Sit down and I'll serve up supper."

Burr knew she was curious about his past, but she could just stay that way. He had decided talking to her wasn't such a good idea after all. He managed to think of grisly things all through supper, which kept his mind off the woman across the table from him. Or mostly kept his mind off her. She ate like she was starving, not at all like a dainty debutante. She cleaned her plate with a gusto that made him wonder if she did everything—and his mind was picturing all sorts of indiscreet activities—with that sort of relish.

"That was delicious," Lindsey said when she finished.

She made no offer to wash the dishes, not that Burr had thought she would. He didn't suppose a governor's daughter got KP duty too often. He thought about just taking care of them himself, but damn it, he was tired. And he had done the cooking.

"You'll find the dish soap under the sink."

Lindsey stared at him blankly for a moment, until she realized what he was implying. "Oh."

In case she wasn't perfectly clear on what he meant, Burr said, "I cooked, you clean."

"I suppose that's fair." She rose and began clearing the table.

Burr was impressed by her willingness to do her share. Unfortunately, he was unable to sit and be waited on. His mother hadn't allowed it when he was growing up, and he couldn't make himself do it now just to spite a woman who couldn't help the fact she had been raised with a silver spoon in her mouth.

"I'll scrape the dishes," he said. "You wash and I'll dry."

"All right."

She was so careful with the dishes, he knew the job wasn't one she was familiar with. "I don't expect you have to wash dishes in the mansion too often."

"No," she said with a quick grin. "I hadn't realized how much fun it is."

"Fun?" He felt his body draw up tight as he watched the

way she caressed a plate with a cloth hidden by a mound of white soapy bubbles. Then she rubbed the cloth around and around inside a coffee cup. Burr felt his cheeks heat. He had never realized washing dishes could be such a sensuous experience. He threw his towel on the counter and headed for the living room. "We can let the rest dry in the drainer. I'll light a fire. It's getting cool outside."

He knelt down in front of the stone fireplace and dropped his forehead to his knee. In twenty hours he would be free of her. He just had to hold on until then. He busied himself building a fire and soon had it crackling. When he turned around, he found Lindsey sitting cross-legged on the couch behind him.

"This is nice," she said.

Too nice, Burr thought. The fire lit up her eyes and made her skin glow with warmth. He had liked it better when she was fighting him. At least then he was being constantly reminded why getting personally involved with the governor's daughter—an ice princess and a spoiled brat, not to mention the girl with "the bluest eyes in Texas"—was a bad idea.

He sat down where he was and crossed his legs, keeping the distance of the room between them. It wasn't enough, of course. But it would have to do.

"What's it like to live in the spotlight?" he asked.

"You wouldn't like it," she replied.

He raised a brow. "Why not?"

"People who don't know a thing about you are always making judgments about you."

"No, I wouldn't like that. I suppose you believe you've been judged unfairly."

"I'm not what the newspapers say I am," she said.

"And what is that?"

"I'm not arrogant, for one thing. Or coldhearted."

Burr cocked a disbelieving brow but didn't say anything.

"It's just that I don't suffer fools gladly."

"I see."

"I don't think you do," she said in a voice that dripped ice. "There is another side of me, a private side, that no one ever sees."

His lips curled in a mocking smile, which suggested that if she believed what she was saying—about not being arrogant or coldhearted—she didn't see herself very clearly. "I guess I haven't met that other woman yet."

"Nor will you," she said in her haughtiest voice. She rose imperiously. "I'm tired. I think I'll go to bed now." Then she turned her back on him and stalked to the bedroom, her fanny gloriously displayed in the skintight jeans.

Burr gritted his teeth. Eighteen hours. She would be gone then, and he would never have to lay eyes on her again. He stayed where he was until he was sure she had the bedroom door closed. Then he rose and settled himself on the couch, using a pillow and the afghan to make himself a bed. He lay staring at the fire for a long time before he finally fell asleep.

Meanwhile, Lindsey was finding it impossible to relax. She didn't want to turn off the lamp, but it had a high-wattage bulb that flooded the room with light. When she tried the dark, it was too frightening. Memories of her kidnapping returned, of waking up in the hotel room, and the deaths of the two villains Burr had been forced to kill. She wanted to go home, to return to the somewhat normal life she had led before all this had happened.

She kept remembering Burr's accusations about her character. If she had been disdainful of the men she met, it was because they treated her like some stone goddess, not a flesh-and-blood woman. Or they were so puffed up with their own consequence they expected her to fall gratefully at their feet. Or they were more interested in her father's political power than in her.

Burr fit none of those neat categories. He wasn't intimidated by her position, and in his arms she was anything but a woman of stone. Her father's power had failed to influence him. She found it amazing and utterly frustrating that a man she found so intriguing seemed to be doing his level best to ignore her!

Her attraction to Burr surprised her more than a little. After all, he was a gang member from Houston who had somehow become a Texas Ranger. And he certainly looked the part.

Appearances.

Lindsey, who had spent her life being judged by her looks, was appalled to realize she had been equally judgmental of Burr's outward trappings. There must be more to him than what showed on the surface. Otherwise, why had she been so drawn to him?

Maybe she found Burr so fascinating because he was different, because he came from the wrong side of the tracks, because he was dangerous. Burr possessed a different kind of power than her father wielded, but there was no doubt Burr Covington was a powerful man. And one who was far more likely to get himself shot than any politician or businessman or financier she could have chosen to fall in love with. And yet, she had been willing to give in to the powerful attraction she felt toward him.

He had made it clear he wasn't interested.

That was another totally new experience for Lindsey Major, debutante and governor's daughter. Normally, men in love with her and begged for her favor. She refused them; they didn't refuse her. She felt humbled, humiliated, and hurt by the Ranger's rejection of her.

Those feelings lasted about as long as it took Lindsey to acknowledge them. They were replaced almost instantaneously by annoyance and determination. She had spent a lifetime using her famous eyes to cajole, entreat and demand what she wanted and rarely failed to get her own way. She didn't want Burr Covington, but she did want a little revenge to assuage her ego. It would be a simple matter to get him to admit he wanted her and then refuse his advances.

Lindsey figured she had about seventeen hours to bring Burr Covington to his knees.

Chapter 4

LINDSEY WOKE TO A STEADY thudding sound, which she finally recognized as an ax striking wood. She got out of bed, crossed to the curtainless window and looked out onto the backyard of the cabin.

Burr was dressed in nothing but a pair of worn jeans, and goose bumps rose on her arms at the sight of him. He had shaved, and she was surprised to see that he looked almost handsome. The broken nose gave his face character, she decided. His hair, free of the ponytail, was plastered to his forehead by sweat and hung in damp curls on his bare shoulders.

He had been working hard enough splitting logs that his muscular torso glistened. Her gaze was drawn to a crystal drop of liquid as it rolled downward across a washboard belly toward his navel. She noticed the scabbed-over cut near his ribs where Epifanio had slashed him with his knife. It wasn't the only mark on his body. There was also a scar near his collarbone that looked suspiciously like a healed bullet wound. She wondered whether he had gotten it as a kid in a Houston gang, or during his duties as a Texas Ranger.

As she watched, he paused and wiped his forehead with a bandanna he pulled from a rear pocket of his jeans.

And noticed her staring at him from the window.

She leapt back out of sight, then realized that was foolish, since he had already seen her. She took a deep breath, shoved the window open and leaned out, unaware that the V-necked T-shirt she was wearing gave Burr a revealing glimpse of female pulchritude. "Good morning," she called.

"There's coffee and cereal in the kitchen," Burr replied curtly. He began swinging the ax again.

She had been dismissed.

Whatever second thoughts Lindsey might have harbored about her plan to bring Burr Covington to his knees flew out the window along with a fly that had been buzzing by her ear. So he thought he could ignore her, did he?

You're being childish about this, Lindsey.

Am I?

The man is only trying to do his job.

That Ranger has insulted me for the last time.

He doesn't strike me as the kind of man who'd ever kowtow to a woman.

Just wait. I haven't been labeled the girl with the bluest eyes in Texas for the past seven years without learning a few things about how to manipulate the male of the species.

Lindsey stripped off the overlarge T-shirt she had slept in and took a quick shower. Then she put on the T-shirt, jeans and tennis shoes Burr had bought for her in town, using some tissues to cushion the blister on her heel.

She didn't normally have more than toast and coffee for breakfast, but the colorful box of sugar-coated kids' cereal on the table looked tempting. She poured herself a bowl, doused it with milk, then surprised herself by eating ravenously. Maybe being kidnapped had given her an appetite. As she munched the last few bites of cereal, Lindsey pondered how she could best seduce the Ranger.

Now you're going to seduce *him?*

How else am I going to lay him low?

How about an intellectual argument?

Somehow that wouldn't be the same.

It sure sounds safer than bearding the lion in his den.

He may look like a lion, but by the time I'm through with him, he'll be following me around like Mary's little lamb.

It dawned on Lindsey that while she had gathered a large male following over the years, she had done nothing purposely to garner their attention, other than having blue eyes, of course. Unfortunately, Burr hadn't fallen under her spell. For the first time, she was going to have to do something other than flutter her eyelashes to attract a man. Since everything else about her was rather ordinary, she wasn't sure exactly what she was going to use for bait. Maybe having an intellectual discussion with Burr wasn't such a bad idea after all.

Burr was immediately aware of Lindsey when she headed out the back door toward him. She had a graceful walk without the limp. Her hair was tied up in a ponytail that made her look a lot younger and more approachable. She wasn't wearing any makeup, either. She looked about twenty and as innocent as a lamb. However, he knew that wasn't possible. A woman like Lindsey Major was sure to have put a few notches in her bedpost. Not that it was any of his business. Besides, having been around more than a little himself, he was in no position to be throwing stones at glass houses.

"Is there anything I can do to help?" Lindsey asked when she reached Burr's side.

"I need to haul some of this wood inside, but otherwise, I'm done here."

"I'd be glad to help with that, but do you suppose we could go for a walk first?"

Burr's gaze shot to her feet. "Are you going to be all right in those shoes?"

"If not, I'll just take them off and go barefoot."

Burr noticed Lindsey was looking everywhere but at him. He set down the ax and mopped his chest and back and under his arms with the T-shirt he had taken off when he had started working.

An enchanting flush rose on Lindsey's face.

Surely this isn't the first time she's seen a man working without a shirt! Burr thought. But she was clearly affected by the sight of him, so he stuck his arms in the plaid Western shirt with folded-up sleeves that had come off at the same time as the T-shirt and buttoned a couple of the buttons.

"I'm ready when you are," he said.

She gave him a gamine smile and headed off toward a cluster of pecan trees in the distance that surrounded a pond deep enough to swim in. He followed after her, wondering why she was being so friendly all of a sudden. He didn't think she had changed her opinion of him overnight, so he was naturally suspicious of her intentions.

He kept his eyes on her, which was easy, considering how her fanny moved in the tight-fitting jeans. There was a sexy little sway to her walk that was as enticing as any perfume he had ever smelled. He realized that if she had walked off a cliff, he probably would have followed her over the edge. The sunshine did something magical to her hair, revealing a dozen different shades from red-gold to golden chestnut. He saw the pleasure on her face as she closed her eyes and tilted her head back, basking in the sunlight.

Burr felt his body responding to the woman in front of him. More disturbing, however, was the way his mind recorded all the sensual data about her. As a Ranger, he was used to making snap judgments about people based on their actions. The way she walked told him she liked being a woman, and that she had a great deal of self-confidence. The sun-streaked hair told him she spent a lot of time outdoors, and that she probably had an expensive hairdresser. And the way she turned her face up to the sun told him she was a sensual person, ready to greet with open arms whatever life had to offer.

He tried to make that evaluation of Lindsey Major mesh with what he had read about her and what he had experienced so far in her company. The pictures didn't match.

"Penny for your thoughts?"

Burr hadn't even realized Lindsey had stopped. She was facing him with her hands on her hips. He took one look at the beautiful woman in front of him and said, "Why aren't you married?"

"I don't think that's any of your business."

"I suppose not. I just wondered why a beautiful woman like you hasn't found herself a husband and settled down to raise a family."

"I've already got a family."

Burr frowned. "I don't understand."

Lindsey turned and started walking toward the trees again, and Burr fell into stride beside her.

"Since the Turk killed my mother five years ago, I've been responsible for raising my younger brother, Carl, and my sister, Stella."

"Seems to me your father ought to be doing that."

She turned and gave him a bittersweet smile. "He doesn't have the time. He's a public servant who takes his duties seriously. I also act as my father's hostess at dinners. You can see why I don't have time to go hunting for a husband."

"I wouldn't think you'd have to go hunting," Burr said frankly.

Lindsey glanced sideways at Burr, and his heart jumped. Her eyes seemed to invite all kinds of things he knew she couldn't

possibly intend. Her next words suggested she meant everything her sultry gaze had conveyed.

"I haven't met anyone I was interested in getting to know."
She paused. "Until you."

Burr stopped in his tracks. He was used to keeping his feelings to himself, but it took a great deal of effort to keep the
astonishment—not to mention the suspicion—off his face. "I
find that a little hard to believe."

"You're...different."

Burr smirked. "I see. Is it the broken nose or the tattoo you
find so fascinating?"

"That's not fair!" Lindsey retorted.

The heat in her face told him he had hit the nail on the head.

"I'm sure there's more to you than your appearance sug-
gests," she said, compounding her error.

Burr laughed out loud.

"I was trying to *compliment* you!"

"I don't think I've ever been damned so well by such faint
praise."

"What I meant is that I don't think I've seen the real Burr
Covington yet, and I'm curious what's behind the 'bad boy'
facade."

"What you see is what you get."

She shook her head, sending her ponytail swinging in the
breeze. "I'm convinced there's more to you than meets the eye,
and I'm determined to get to know the real Burr Covington
before the day ends."

"What's the sense of that?" Burr asked. "After I return you to your father this afternoon, we'll never see each other again."

"It doesn't have to be that way," Lindsey said in a quiet voice.

Burr's lips curled in a cynical smile. "What kind of rig are you running, Blue Eyes? What is it you want from me?"

She looked at him with those stunning eyes, and he felt his heart skip a beat. He hadn't expected to be as vulnerable as the rest of the pack that worshipped the bluest eyes in Texas. But he found himself wondering what it would be like to wake up to those eyes every morning for the rest of his life. He shook his head to break free of her spell.

"Well?" he demanded. "What is it you want?"

"I'm attracted to you," she blurted. "I thought—"

"Oh, no, you don't. I am not, I repeat, *not* getting involved with the governor's daughter. I'm supposed to be guarding you, for Christ's sake!"

He didn't know quite how it happened, but she took the few steps to reach him and laid her hands on his chest and looked up at him, her lips parted.

"I want you to kiss me," she said in a husky voice.

Burr's hands clamped down on Lindsey's arms so hard they were liable to be bruised when he let go. But, hell, better that than the other alternative, which was to kiss the woman— which he had to admit had crossed his mind as a potentially pleasant experience—and damn the consequences.

"We are *not* going to do this."

"Why not?"

"Because you are who you are, and I am who I am."

"That's not a very good reason to deny ourselves."

"Then I'll give you a few more. I grew up in a gang in Houston—you grew up as Texas royalty. I live life in the trenches—you amble along up top. And this situation is only temporary. You wouldn't look twice at me if we weren't stuck here together."

Her eyes flashed, and she stabbed a forefinger against his chest. "Hogwash. The only thing that matters is whether or not you're as attracted to me as I am to you. Are you?"

He let her go and forked a hand through his hair in agitation. "All right, I'm attracted to you! Is that what you wanted to hear?"

She grinned from ear to ear. "It's a start."

"Just remember you asked for this."

Burr captured her in his arms and lowered his mouth to hers. He felt her catch fire when he put his tongue in her mouth to taste her, but he didn't stop there. He had wanted to hold her breasts since he had first caught sight of them. He shoved his hand up under her T-shirt and palmed her flesh. She made a sound of protest before arching into his hand. He used his other hand to hold her close while he rubbed himself against her with a body that was stone hard. When he let her go at last, there was a stunned look on her face.

He took a step back and let out a shuddering breath. "Is that what you were after, Blue Eyes? Be sure it's what you want before you start playing games with me again." He didn't recognize his voice. It was harsh and grated like a rusty gate.

"I wasn't…I didn't mean…" Her denials fell flat because she had goaded him, and she had meant to provoke exactly the response she had gotten. Only the encounter had been far more devastating for her than she had imagined. She felt shattered. Overwhelmed. Aroused. And afraid to act on what she was feeling for fear of the consequences.

"Now you know the real difference between the two of us. I'm not into playing games, Blue Eyes."

"And you think I am?"

"Aren't you?"

"I wasn't thinking about the differences between us when you were kissing me."

"That's good, because when I look at you I see a woman I want to get so deep inside I can't see daylight, a woman I want underneath me panting and scratching and as eager for me as I am for her. How about it, Blue Eyes? You ready for that?"

Burr watched Lindsey's jaw drop. Then she whirled and fled back to the cabin as fast as her legs could carry her.

You're a damn fool, Covington. She was asking for it. You should have given it to her. Why did you scare her off?

She doesn't know what she's getting into. I would be taking advantage of her at a vulnerable time.

She came on to you.

She's a woman who doesn't know what the hell she wants.

You had your chance to make love to her and you blew it.

Yeah. Sometimes those are the breaks.

Acknowledging his folly didn't make Burr feel any better.

He headed toward the pond situated among the pecan trees. He needed a dip to cool off. He couldn't remember a time when he had been so turned on by a woman. Why the hell did it have to be her? They had nothing in common. There was absolutely no future for the two of them. He simply wasn't the kind of man who chased after windmills.

LINDSEY HAD BEEN SHOCKED and not a little shaken by Burr's prompt and devastating response to her sexual invitation. She was used to a more civilized male creature, one who would ask permission and accept limits. Burr had given her fair warning and then taken what he wanted from her.

Not that she had protested much…or at all. In fact, she had quickly found herself a willing participant in anything and everything he'd had in mind to offer her. And she had to admit there was every bit as much give as there was take in what he had done.

So why did you run, Lindsey?

The answer to that was simple. She had been frightened by the powerful feelings Burr incited. She had no explanation for her attraction to the Ranger. She only knew she wanted to feel his arms around her, wanted to put her arms around him and hold him close. She was as appalled as she was astounded that she could be so attracted to a man like him. He didn't mince words; he didn't play games. He had a tattoo, for heaven's sake! But his need for her, his intense desire, was a strong aphrodisiac.

She had thought she could tease the lion and escape unharmed. But this beast had sharp teeth and dangerous claws that could drag her down and destroy her if she let him.

She remembered the avid look in Burr's eyes as his hand had cupped her breast. It was impossible to forget the taste of him, the rough feel of his tongue as he probed her mouth, the way his teeth caught her lower lip, and how her body had drawn up tight as he sucked on it. Her hips had met his thrusts and sought more of the delicious feelings as he brushed against her through two layers of soft denim.

Lindsey had fooled around in high school, done a little petting, but she had never gone "all the way." Somehow, the things her mother had told her about saving herself for marriage had made sense. Since she had expected to meet her future husband in college, that hadn't seemed like such a long time to wait.

Then her mother had been killed, and her life had been turned upside down. For the past five years she had lived as celibate as a nun. Perhaps it was those years of deprivation that had caused her to respond so wildly to Burr. Or maybe grown-up hormones were more powerful than the teenage ones. All she knew was that what she had felt with Burr far surpassed anything she had ever experienced in the past.

Lindsey felt confused and still half-aroused and wasn't sure what her next move ought to be. Maybe the smart move was to make no move at all. She would let Burr set the tone for the rest of the day. Much as it irked her to concede any battle, she knew when she was outgunned. It would be better to retreat while she still could.

She spent the next hour carting firewood into the house and

wondering where Burr was. When he returned, she realized he must have gone swimming. His hair was slicked back and his skin was pearled with drops of water. She had a fierce urge to taste his skin, to lick up those crystal drops. She forced herself to stay where she was.

"You took a swim."

"Yeah."

They stared at each other for a moment without speaking. Then Burr said, "It's time for me to call in. If we're lucky, Hector's been picked up, and you can go home."

Lindsey was torn between wanting to go home and wanting more time with Burr. She had been attracted to him because he was so different from the men she usually met. She felt certain that if she didn't discover the man behind the mask before Burr Covington, Texas Ranger, dropped her off in front of the governor's mansion and said goodbye, she never would. Lindsey found that a very painful thought.

"You won't get any crazy ideas while I'm gone, like walking to the road, will you?" Burr said.

"No. I'll wait here."

"I shouldn't be more than an hour. You'll be safe here." He reached out a hand and tucked an errant curl behind her ear. The instant he realized what he had done, Burr withdrew his hand. A moment later he captured her head between his hands and kissed her hard on the mouth. "Be here when I get back."

"I will."

Chapter 5

LINDSEY STEPPED OUT onto the porch as Burr shut off the Jaguar's engine. "What's the news?"

Burr joined her on the porch, his face solemn. "Hector escaped the trap that was set for him. The captain thinks he may have left the country for South America."

"Now what?"

"The captain says we stay here," Burr said flatly.

"How long?"

"Until the Turk's sentence is carried out."

"That's four days!"

"I know."

Lindsey was amazed that she didn't feel more disappointed. In fact, what she felt was elated. She had four more days to find out everything there was to know about Burr Covington. Four more days to figure out the source of the riotous feelings that had bombarded her when Burr had so solemnly announced they were stuck together for a while longer.

To her consternation, Burr completely avoided her the rest of the day, which wasn't easy, since they both had to eat and sleep in the cabin. Somehow, he arranged it so she ate before he did and retired to bed before he returned from taking a late evening walk.

Lindsey lay in bed chewing on a fingernail. Maybe Burr had the right idea. Maybe it was better if they didn't get to know each other. She tried to imagine introducing Burr to her father as someone she cared about and had a pretty good idea what he would say: she was suffering from some kind of kidnapping syndrome and had fallen for the man who had rescued her from the bad guys.

Lindsey admitted she had something like an adolescent crush on Burr. She refused to dignify her desire to have him kiss her and hold her in his arms with any other label. How could it be more than infatuation? She had only known the man for forty-eight hours. She wasn't even sure she liked him. But there was no doubt she was physically attracted to him.

It occurred to her that perhaps the best way to get over her physical attraction to Burr was to find out what kind of man he really was. Personality flaws were bound to show up that would make him repugnant to her as a lover. Her crush would die a quick death under the weight of his unattractive character traits.

However, her plan required her to spend time in Burr Covington's company, discovering the unattractive man behind the fascinating "bad boy" facade. Which meant she had to find a way to keep Burr from disappearing before she had a chance to ask him a few questions. She decided to rise early the next morning and make a breakfast he wouldn't be able to resist sharing.

THE SMELL OF FRYING BACON woke Burr.

"Breakfast is ready!" Lindsey called from the kitchen. "Come and get it!"

Burr wasn't a morning person. His mind didn't start functioning until he had washed the cobwebs out with a shower, and he needed several cups of coffee before he could face the day. He met the call to come directly to the breakfast table with wariness. He needed his wits about him to deal with Lindsey Major.

He had managed to avoid any contact with the governor's daughter the previous day, but if he was any judge of the situation, he wasn't going to be allowed to repeat his disappearing act. He rubbed a weary hand across his bristly jaw. He hadn't gotten much sleep because he had spent the night dreaming in lurid detail of what it would be like to make love to her.

He struggled upright, shoving the afghan off his bare legs. He pressed his palms against eyelids he would have sworn were endowed with spikes the way they scraped against his eyeballs. Maybe if he got up on the wrong side of the bed—make that couch—and let Miss Major see him at his worst, it would discourage her.

Burr felt a grin struggling to break free. If Miss Major wanted him, she was going to get him. Warts and all.

He pulled on his jeans and zipped them, but didn't bother buttoning them. They caught on his hipbones. He headed for the kitchen barefoot, scratching his naked chest, his hair stuck up every whichaway and a dark stubble on his cheeks and chin.

When he reached the kitchen doorway he grabbed hold of the molding above his head and held on, letting his body sag slightly forward. "Got any coffee?"

Lindsey turned toward him, and he nearly laughed out loud at the look on her face. Her features ran the gamut between disappointment and delight. Clearly she was glad he had joined her for breakfast. Equally clearly, she hadn't seen a man in his condition at the breakfast table.

He let go of the molding and took the three steps necessary to sit at the table, which had been adorned with china and silverware—his mismatched plates, chipped cups and stainless-steel flatware—in a way that would have pleased Miss Manners. He leaned his head on his hand and blatantly stared at Lindsey while she filled his coffee cup. "Thanks."

"How would you like your eggs?" she asked.

"Over easy."

She cracked a couple of eggs into the pan she had used to cook the bacon. He noticed she watched the eggs as though they might run away and ignored his presence in the room.

"This is a nice surprise," he said.

She looked over her shoulder at him somewhat nervously. "I thought this might be a way to repay you in some small measure for all you've done for me."

Burr grunted. "You don't owe me anything. I'm just doing my job."

"It may not seem like much to you, but I can't help thinking what might have happened to me at the hotel if you hadn't been there."

He saw her hands were trembling but resisted the urge to get up and go comfort her. Black knights didn't comfort ladies fair. He watched her visibly calm herself.

"I thought maybe we could walk down to the pond after breakfast," she said.

Burr knew why he wanted to spend time with her. What made no sense was why she apparently wanted to spend time with him. He had already warned her what would happen if she exhibited an interest in his attentions. She was damn well going to get them! Well, she was a big girl, and she knew the consequences of playing with fire. He figured he might as well enjoy her company while he could. It was a choice he might not have made if he hadn't still been fuzzy with sleep.

Almost a full minute after Lindsey had asked him to go walking with her to the pond, he replied, "Yeah, I'll go with you." After all, he was supposed to be keeping an eye on her.

"Do you suppose it would be all right if I went for a swim?"

Burr had just taken a gulp of hot coffee, and he choked and sputtered as a vivid picture rose before him of what Lindsey would look like with water dripping off her naked body. He felt his groin tighten with anticipation. "Sure. Why not?"

Burr was surprised when Lindsey set a plate of eggs, bacon and toast in front of him that were cooked to perfection. He gave her a look of admiration.

"I took some classes in French cooking. We practiced a lot with eggs," she explained as she joined him on the other side of the table with a plate of her own.

They ate in uncomfortable silence, which Lindsey finally broke when she said, "I was wondering how someone who belonged to a street gang ended up as a Texas Ranger."

Burr hadn't told the story to very many people. Maybe if Lindsey knew the truth about him, she would back off and leave him alone. Maybe a dose of reality would cure what ailed her.

"My father died when I was two," he began. "My mother went to work as a waitress in a truck stop outside Houston. She didn't have any family, so she brought me with her to work and kept me behind the counter. I sort of grew up there."

"In a truck stop?"

Burr's lips curved at the look of horror and disbelief on Lindsey's face. It was just dawning on her that they came from two different worlds.

"It wasn't such a bad place. The truckers sort of adopted me, but none of them ever stayed around very long, so I never got attached to any of them. The problems started when I turned fifteen. The Cobras—that was the gang I eventually joined—all showed up one day at the truck stop. I was fascinated by them. They talked hip and looked cool. Most of all, they were a family.

"At the time, I needed to belong. So I joined up. I had to do a lot of things, initiation rites, before I could be a part of the gang. It was mostly petty thievery, vandalism, that sort of thing. And they beat you up to see if you could take it."

"That's terrible!"

Burr shrugged. "That part wasn't any fun. But afterward I was one of them, so it seemed worth it. Once I was in, I got the tattoo." He brushed his fingertips absently against the coiled black snake.

"There's no telling what might have happened to me if my mother hadn't married a Houston cop." He smiled in remembrance. "Joe Bertram came into the truck stop to investigate the theft of some video equipment—which I had stolen. The minute he and my mom laid eyes on each other they fell in love. I've never seen anything like it.

"Joe became my stepfather a month later. You could say my life of crime came to a rather abrupt end. He laid down the law and made me toe the line. He forced me to quit the Cobras. When I look back on it now, I can see he was a pretty terrific guy. At the time, I hated his guts.

"The long and the short of it is, the week after I graduated from the University of Texas at Austin with a degree in business, he was killed in the line of duty."

He paused and swallowed hard.

"I didn't even know I loved him till I heard the news." Burr turned away so she wouldn't see the tears that stung his eyes. "I felt cheated that I had lost him just when I was starting to appreciate him. And I felt bad that I hadn't ever thanked him. I figured one way I could repay him for all he'd done for me was to become a cop myself.

"Fortunately, the Rangers provide a natural stomping ground for renegades and loners like me. I put in my time as a cop and applied for the Rangers as soon as I was eligible." He spread his hands wide. "Here I am."

Burr had spent his life trying to make up to his stepfather for the trouble he had given him. In all these years he had never forgiven himself for the hateful things he had said to the man who had given him such tough love, even though his mother had assured him that his stepfather had forgiven him—had known his stepson cared for him—long before his death.

"Where's your mother now?" Lindsey asked.

"She died two years ago."

"So you're all alone?"

"I don't have any family left, if that's what you're asking."

"Why haven't you married?"

"I suppose I never found the right woman."

"What would she be like?"

"I haven't really thought about it. There's no such thing as perfection, so I guess I'd settle for a woman I loved who loved me back."

"Sounds pretty simple."

"Not many women want to be married to a law enforcement officer."

Lindsey nodded. "I suppose they don't want to wind up widows. I can understand that."

"And agree with the sentiment?"

"I lost my mother to violence. I live every day with the fear that an assassin will kill my father. So, no, I don't think I've ever imagined myself marrying a man whose life would constantly be on the line."

Burr rarely pondered his mortality. He couldn't afford to because it might distract him from the job he had to do. But he couldn't deny he was involved in a dangerous profession, and he couldn't blame a woman who considered that risk when choosing a husband. Even if it put him squarely out of the running.

While they were talking, Burr had finished the food in front of him and drunk a second cup of coffee. When Lindsey started clearing the table, he rose and took his plate from her "You cooked, I clean, remember?"

She gave him a quick look from lowered lashes before saying, "I'll go change into something I can swim in."

Burr wondered what she would find to serve as a swimsuit and was rewarded when she arrived back in the kitchen a few minutes later with a sight that made his whole body go taut.

Her face looked fresh and innocent as she glanced quickly up at him from blue eyes masked by dark, lush lashes. Her mouth was slightly parted, and he could see her breasts rise and fall in a T-shirt that made it plain she wasn't wearing a bra. Her hair was a silky mane of gold that spilled over her shoulders and begged for a man's hands to grasp handfuls of it to pull her close. The T-shirt was tied in a knot above a pair of his cut-off jeans that revealed the length of her tanned, shapely legs.

It was an outfit designed to drive a man's imagination wild. Burr turned toward the sink so she wouldn't see that his body had promptly responded to the sexual invitation she had unconsciously thrown out.

"I'll be finished here in a minute and we can go," Burr said in a voice that was surprisingly husky.

"I'll wait for you on the porch."

Burr was grateful for the respite to get his libido back under control.

Whoa, boy! That sexy little siren is the governor's daughter!

She's also a very desirable woman.

Who's off limits!

Why?

You know damn well why! She wouldn't look at you twice if the circumstances were other than what they are. What kind of future could the two of you have together?

So what's wrong with a little fling?

With the governor's daughter? Get a grip, man. Think of the consequences!

Burr tried to imagine the possible consequences of slaking his lust with Lindsey Major. The mind boggled. Better to grit his teeth and bear the pain of unsatisfied passion. In the long run that was the smart move.

His resolve lasted until Lindsey came up from her first dip in the creek in the wet T-shirt. Her nipples had peaked from the cold, and he was treated to a sight that made idiots of adolescent males at beach parties. Burr told himself he was an intelligent grown man who knew better than to succumb to such riveting sights.

When Lindsey called, "Why don't you join me?" he responded with a muttered oath and stood his ground.

"I promise the water isn't too cold," she teased.

Maybe that was what he needed, Burr thought, a dip in some cold water. He yanked off his black T-shirt and sat down to remove his boots and socks. Then, still wearing his jeans, he strode into the icy water.

He wasn't consciously heading for Lindsey at first. Not until she began to back away from him. She should have known better than to run. A hunter could never resist the chase.

He saw the teasing smile on her face begin to fade as she realized he was coming for her.

"Burr...Burr..."

When she turned and raced for the bank, he ran after her. He caught her in the grassy verge and pulled her down. They rolled several times before he pinned her beneath him.

She didn't fight, but lay panting, her eyes wide, her body pliant. She slicked her tongue over her lips, leaving them wet. Her gaze met his, and he waited for a sign that she wanted to be freed. It didn't come.

He lowered his mouth to hers, tasting the dampness, and heard her moan low in her throat. He pressed his hips down and felt her arch upward to meet him. This time he groaned.

"Lindsey, if you don't want this, say so now."

"I want you, Burr. Please, don't stop."

He had the wet T-shirt and shorts off her moments later and shimmied out of his wet jeans a moment after that. He settled himself between her thighs and then raised himself up on his elbows to look at her.

"You're so beautiful!" He watched the flush steal up her throat to stain her cheeks. Her eyes were closed, the lashes a fan of coal across rose-petal skin. "Look at me, Lindsey."

Lindsey had closed her eyes on purpose, not wanting Burr to focus on them because she had been judged for so long by their uniqueness. She wanted to be appreciated for who she was inside, not because she had the bluest eyes in Texas. She raised her lids slowly, first to a slit, then wider as she saw the admiration and approval in his tender gaze.

He brushed his thumb across her cheek and then slid it across her parted lips. She dipped her tongue out to taste him and heard his hiss of pleasure. His dark eyes seemed to bore into her, seeking the person within. She willed him to see her as she was—innocent, needing him, wanting him, not quite frightened, but anxious about the unknown.

They didn't speak again. At least not with words. He caressed her skin as though it were the most fragile silk, and finally lowered his mouth to suckle her breast as his hands explored her body.

Lindsey bit her lip to keep from crying out, but couldn't suppress the guttural sounds that escaped her throat. She had never imagined it could be like this, never imagined the powerful response her body could have to the touch of a callused male hand. His mouth kept moving over her, up to her throat, then to her ear, inciting pleasure wherever it roamed. She felt a shiver of desire when his teeth nipped her shoulder, and sought out his skin with her mouth to return the pleasure.

"Your skin is so soft," he mused. "And your hair." His hand tightened around a fistful of the silky stuff and pulled her head back to expose her throat for his kisses.

Lindsey was overwhelmed with feelings. She responded with the desperation she felt, tunneling her hands into Burr's hair and grasping hold to keep his mouth where it was as her body arched beneath his. She relished his groan of delight as she brushed against his shaft.

His invasion came swiftly and without warning. She stiffened and cried out.

Burr froze. He didn't pull away, merely lifted himself on his palms to stare into Lindsey's face. He caught the remnants of pain in her eyes. And the growing exhilaration.

"You should have told me," he said in a harsh voice.

"Would you have done this if I had?"

"Hell, no!"

"Then I'm glad I didn't say anything."

Burr let out his breath in a sigh. "I hurt you."

"The pain is gone now." She still felt stretched, and her body ached, but that was bearable. And she knew the worst was over. "Please don't stop."

Burr snorted. "I'm not about—"

She put her fingertips across his mouth to silence him and let her eyes plead for what she wanted. She raised herself enough to replace her fingertips with her mouth. Her tongue traced the crease of his lips and when he parted them, slid inside. She moaned with delight as Burr's tongue forced hers back into her mouth and claimed the honey to be found there.

His hands cupped her shoulders and pressed her back down as his body began to move in tandem with hers. His thrusts were slow and easy at first, but as she began to answer him, his body plunged deeper, seeking pleasure, giving it, until they were slick from sweat, until their bodies begged for air, until each cried out as he spent his seed within her.

CONSEQUENCES.

It was the first thought that popped into Lindsey's head as she lay atop Burr, still gasping for air, totally enervated. They hadn't used any kind of protection. She knew better, and he must certainly be aware of the dangers of unprotected sex.

"Do you…? Have you…?"

"It's a little late for that, Blue Eyes, don't you think?" Burr said in a quiet voice. "But, no, I don't have anything you can catch. And I don't expect, under the circumstances, that I'm going to catch anything from you. That leaves pregnancy. Is this the right—or wrong—time of the month?"

Lindsey's face was beet red. She kept her eyes lowered. "I just got over… It's the wrong time of month for me to get pregnant," she blurted.

He pulled her close to his chest and held her there. "Thank goodness for that, anyway." He was quiet for a long time before he said, "Why me?"

"It's not what you're thinking."

"What am I thinking?"

"That this is just a fling."

"Isn't it?"

Lindsey was silent for a moment. Is that what Burr had thought? That she just wanted to have sex with him for the fun of it? That she didn't care for him as a person? But, honestly, what else could he think? They barely knew each other. They were strangers. The likelihood of them continuing any kind of relationship once she returned to the governor's mansion was small indeed. So why had she allowed—no, honest, Lindsey—*encouraged* this to happen?

"I don't know what it is," Lindsey admitted. "I think I wanted to see if I could make you want me. I didn't realize until…until you caught me that I wanted to be caught. And then…" She shrugged. "I'm not sorry it happened, though. I have feelings for you that are…" *Stronger than I'm willing to admit even to myself, let alone to you.* She didn't dare speak of love. It was an absurdity under the circumstances.

"No regrets?"

She shook her head. "It had to happen sometime, and—"

Burr rolled her off him and was on his feet an instant later. "And I was convenient," he finished in a hard voice. "Don't fool yourself into thinking I'm something I'm not. I'll always be a man more used to walking alleys than streets. There's no getting rid of my past, like there's no getting rid of the tattoo on my arm. And if it's all the same to you, Blue Eyes, I've had enough of being a convenience."

Burr was aware of a tightness in his chest. It had dawned on him that he would give anything to have a woman like Lindsey for his own, to hold and to love. He couldn't stand the thought of another man touching her, loving her. Only, he had no right to those feelings. Their situation wasn't real; it was contrived. How could he even think about proposing to the governor's daughter?

His hurt turned to anger when he realized the situation Lindsey had put him in. He was furious she hadn't told him that he would be the first man to make love to her. He sure as hell hadn't been thinking in terms of forever, as any woman who had saved her virginity as long as Lindsey had must have been. He knew, even if she didn't, that the governor's daughter wasn't going to marry a former Houston gang member, a man with a snake tattoo on his arm and an earring in his ear, even if he was a Texas Ranger.

"You should have waited for the right man to come along, Blue Eyes, instead of wasting your innocence on me."

She had hurt him, Lindsey realized, and he had snapped back with something equally hurtful. She sought some way to make amends. "I didn't mean—"

"I know what I am, Miss Major, and what I'm not. The question is, do you?"

"Now wait just a minute, Burr Covington," Lindsey said.

"You can't use that snake tattoo or your broken nose to scare me off! You aren't so tough."

"Oh, yeah?"

"Yeah!" She poked him in the chest with her forefinger. "There's a fellow inside there somewhere who makes my heart beat fast, a guy who leaves me breathless. So there!"

Burr was tempted by her speech to take her back in his arms. But he already had his wet jeans on, which helped immensely to dampen his ardor and keep him from doing something that foolish. "Get dressed."

"I won't let you ignore me." Lindsey reached out and stopped him from buttoning his jeans. "I wanted *you* to make love to me, Burr. You."

Burr grabbed her wrists to keep her from touching him. His body was on fire, and he knew if he let her arguments sway him, he would be the one who got burned. If he let himself believe her, he would start thinking about a future together, and he knew better than that. "Get dressed," he repeated. "I can't leave you out here alone."

He glared at her while she tugged on her cut-offs and pulled her soggy T-shirt over her head. The flimsy cotton did nothing to hide her lush body, and he felt his loins tighten at the sight of her nipples through the thin cloth. The minute she was dressed, he grabbed her wrist. "Let's go."

"How can I make you believe that I mean what I'm saying?" Lindsey said as he dragged her along beside him.

"I should have known better than to let myself lose control like that," he muttered.

"I do care about you. I—"

He jerked her to a stop. "Don't you dare use words like that when you don't mean them! You have no idea what it means to care about anyone but yourself. You're exactly what the papers call you—a pretty pair of blue eyes without any substance behind them!"

"How do you know what I feel?" she cried. "Why are you acting like an insensitive, uncaring brute?"

"So now I'm a brute? You're the one who came after me, so what does that make you, lady? You asked for it, and I gave it to you!"

"Oh, you…you…" Lindsey was so furious and hurt, nearly blinded by the tears she was furiously blinking back, that she couldn't find an epithet bad enough to use on him.

"Who are you to be judging me," Burr demanded with a sneer, "when you don't have a life of your own? You're a substitute wife for your father, a substitute mother for your siblings. You wouldn't know how to be yourself, because there's nothing more to Lindsey Major than a pair of pretty blue eyes."

Lindsey was appalled at how close Burr had come to describing her life and enraged that he had rejected her because of it. "And you'll never outgrow your roots," she taunted back. "You'll always be a street hood at heart."

They stood glaring at each other. Each wanting desperately to be the kind of person the other wanted and sure they fell far short of the other's expectations.

Burr wondered what would have happened if they had met under different circumstances, when labels could have been dispensed with, when they could just have been a man and a woman meeting for the first time without the concealing masks they had both worn for so many years.

"Hey, you two, what's the problem?"

Lindsey and Burr turned to stare openmouthed at the man dressed in a ranger uniform who stood on the porch of the cabin.

Burr cleared his throat. "Captain Rogers? What are you doing here?"

"Hector fooled us. He didn't get on that plane to South America, after all. One of our informants saw him and tipped us off. We picked him up a couple of hours ago. You can go home now, Miss Major."

Lindsey turned stricken eyes toward Burr. "I can go home."

"Yes, ma'am," the captain continued, oblivious to the powerful undercurrents between Burr and Lindsey. "Your father's waiting for you at the mansion. I'll give you a lift there."

"I'll give her a ride," Burr said. Unspoken was the knowledge that they would finish their conversation on the way. Only, what was there left to say?

Lindsey shoved a fist against her mouth to keep a sob from escaping and raced into the cabin.

"What the hell did you do to that woman?" Captain Rogers asked.

Loved her. Burr thought. *I just loved her.*

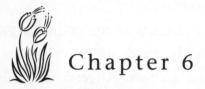 Chapter 6

IN THE FACE OF THE ACCUSATIONS each had made against the other, both Lindsey and Burr remained silent during the first part of the drive back to Austin.

It's over too soon, Lindsey thought.

I never had an even chance with her, Burr thought.

I'm not what he thinks I am.

There's more to me than she knows.

Maybe I need to look more closely at who I am, Lindsey thought.

Maybe I ought to look at myself and see what's really there, Burr thought.

"I never realized before how thoroughly I took my mother's place after she died," Lindsey murmured, her voice barely audible. "At first, after my mother's death, my father was so desolate he couldn't function. I saw a void, and I filled it. I suppose I should have stepped back sooner, but the role was comfortable for me. I felt needed. I *was* needed. Now...I don't know.

Carl and Stella are old enough to resent it when I try to parent them. And my father...I think he wouldn't have the heart to tell me he didn't need my help anymore."

"But you think he could survive now without you?"

Lindsey made a face. "He hired a new secretary last year. She's quite good at what she does."

"I see."

Lindsey was afraid Burr saw too much. "At least I'm willing to admit I need to make a change. What about you? How well do your stepfather's shoes fit, Burr?"

Burr kept his eyes on the road, refusing to meet her gaze "You don't pull any punches, do you, Blue Eyes?" And of course she was right. It was time he figured out whether he was in this line of work for his stepfather's sake...or his own.

Burr had spent so many years giving mental lip service to the idea he was a cop to repay his stepfather, that he hadn't thought about how much he enjoyed his work. He liked being a Texas Ranger; he was good at it. And it was a satisfying job, giving him the independence his soul craved along with the opportunity to serve a noble purpose.

But was the role of Texas Ranger sufficient for the husband of a woman like Lindsey Major? He would never be rich, and his first devotion was to duty. Although he would cherish Lindsey if she were his, there would necessarily be times when his job would take him away from her. It might even kill him. He didn't want to think about how she would feel if that happened.

Lindsey snuck a peek at Burr and wondered what traits he

wanted in a wife. She was beautiful, but what else did she have to offer a husband? She had a great deal of experience as an organizer and a hostess, but somehow she didn't think the wife of a Texas Ranger needed those skills. She was frightened of the danger he lived with day in and day out. Her heart caught in her throat when she admitted the perilous danger of his chosen profession.

Life with a man like Burr would never be easy. But she understood now why her mother had endured the trials and tribulations of life as a politician's wife. Loving, caring, left no choices.

Lindsey stared straight ahead as the interstate flew by, unwilling to speak again because she was afraid all the things she was feeling would pour out of her mouth. Her relationship—if you could call it that—with Burr was over before it had started. She was going back to her world. He was going back to his. Their paths wouldn't cross again, not without some effort on one or both of their parts. She was leaving it up to him to make the first move. That might be old-fashioned, but she wasn't willing to lay her heart on the line without some indication from him that he was willing to do the same.

The governor's mansion was in sight before she finally asked the question that was foremost in her mind. "Will I ever see you again?"

"What would be the point?"

Lindsey looked down at her hands, which were knotted in her lap. "I thought we started something by the river."

"If there are consequences, by all means call me."

Lindsey shot an angry look at Burr. "You know that wasn't what I meant. And I wouldn't call you now even if I were expecting triplets!"

"It wouldn't work," Burr said in a quiet voice. He glanced at her for an instant, then focused on the road in front of him. "You and me, I mean. I think in our case appearances aren't at all deceiving. You're a princess living in an ivory tower, and I'm—"

"Prince Charming. Or you could be."

Burr shook his head and laughed. "Whoever heard of Prince Charming with a snake tattooed on his arm? Can you imagine what your father would say if he saw the two of us together?"

"He wouldn't care."

Burr raised a skeptical brow, and Lindsey conceded, "At least, not after he got to know you."

"Both of us know appearances count, Blue Eyes. Think of the heyday the press would have if the two of us showed up in public together."

"What's printed in newspapers doesn't have to affect us."

"What about your friends? What will they say?"

"If they can't—or won't—accept you as you are, they won't be my friends for long."

Burr sighed. "It won't work, Blue Eyes. We're too different."

"We both want the same thing," Lindsey argued. "Someone to love…someone who'll love us back. We could have that together, Burr. Nothing else matters."

"Now I know you've been living in an ivory tower. We wouldn't have a snowball's chance in hell of surviving the rebuke that would be leveled against us from all directions. Me for stepping out of my place, and you for stooping down from yours. Think of the headlines   Bluest Eyes In Texas To Wed Former Gang Thug, or Texas Ranger Nabs Bluest Eyes In Texas."

"If you don't want me, just say so."

"Wanting you has nothing to do with it! I want you like hell. I'm just trying to be realistic about the situation."

"If your mind's made up, I don't suppose I can change it," Lindsey said. "But I'm stating here and now for the record that I think you're wrong. If you decide you want me bad enough to fight for me, you know where to find me."

She was out of the car and running inside the mansion before he had a chance to stop her. Not that he would have known what to say to her if he had. She was wrong. There was no way they could have a life together. He wasn't Prince Charming. He was an ordinary man with a slightly crooked nose and a snake tattoo and a few scars he had earned along the way. When the governor's blue-eyed daughter had recovered from the trauma of being kidnapped, of being held captive by a Ranger against her will, of being made love to for the first time, she would be glad he had bowed gracefully out of her life.

Lindsey threw herself into her father's embrace and sobbed with relief as his arms tightened securely around her.

"Are you all right, Lindsey?" he asked. "Are you hurt?"

"I'm fine, Dad," she managed between gulps as she fought back her tears. "It's just…it was *awful!* There was so much blood and those two men dead, and Burr… Oh, Dad!"

"I know sweetheart. I know. You'll be fine now. Nothing bad is ever going to happen to you again. I'll see to that." Lindsey heard the remorse in her father's voice that she had been forced to suffer through the kidnapping and his determination to protect her from harm in the future. She could feel the walls closing in on her. It was a gilded cage her father wanted her to inhabit, but it was still a cage. If the governor got his way, she would never see Burr again, that was for sure. A brilliant idea popped into Lindsey's head, and she acted on it.

"If it hadn't been for Lieutenant Covington, I would have been brutalized and blinded before I was murdered. He saved me, Dad. Isn't there something we can do for him? Some way to thank him?"

"I don't know. I'll have to think about it."

"Could we have some sort of ceremony and give him a medal? We could invite him to dinner, too, couldn't we?"

The speculative look her father gave her brought a telltale blush to Lindsey's cheeks.

"You seem to have gotten along pretty well with this Covington fellow."

"He saved my life," Lindsey repeated.

"Hmm."

Lindsey held her breath.

"All right. I'll talk to Captain Rogers and see if a commendation of some sort is appropriate."

"And we'll invite him to dinner?"

"Sure. Why not?"

BURR SLIPPED A FINGER into the collar of his tuxedo shirt and tried to loosen it. He felt like a mustang running with a herd of high-priced Thoroughbreds. He was wearing black cordovan dress shoes instead of boots, and his hair had been trimmed so much it curled at his nape. There was no earring in his ear and the snake tattoo was far out of sight. Except for his broken nose, he looked like most of the other men in tuxedos who had been invited to the governor's mansion for dinner.

Only, he was a fraud. They looked comfortable in the clothes they wore. They smiled and nodded and chatted with ease. He knew the moment he opened his mouth the wrong thing was going to come out. This wasn't his milieu. He would always be more comfortable in alleys than on streets.

He had learned from the captain that this reception in his honor was all Lindsey's idea, supposedly a way to repay him for what he had done.

"I was only doing my job," Burr had protested.

The captain hadn't been willing to take no for an answer. "You're going to dine as the governor's guest, and I don't want to hear any more argument!"

So HERE HE WAS, ALL DRESSED UP and fighting the bit to be somewhere else.

"Hello, stranger."

Burr turned and his breath caught in his throat. He had forgotten how beautiful she was. She was wearing a dress similar in style to the one she had been kidnapped in, only this one was black. He wondered fleetingly if she was wearing a black merry widow beneath it.

She smiled at him as though divining the direction his thoughts had taken. The look in her eyes made him want to haul her off somewhere and kiss her silly. He settled for taking the hand she extended and holding it in his own.

His thumb caressed her wrist, and he felt her pulse leap beneath his fingertips. "It's been a while," he managed to force past his constricted throat.

"Three weeks and two days."

"You've been counting?"

"Haven't you?"

He grinned. "Three weeks, two days, and eight hours."

"I've missed you." Lindsey couldn't take her eyes off Burr. The crisp white shirt contrasted against his tanned skin, and the black tux jacket emphasized his broad shoulders. He looked distinguished, but no less dangerous. For the first time in her very social life, Lindsey was incredibly nervous. She didn't know how to act and took her cues from Burr.

Burr ignored her invitation to admit to feelings that were only trouble. The orchestra at the far end of the ballroom had just begun a waltz, so he asked, "Would you like to dance?"

"I'd love to dance."

He led her into the waltz, a dance he knew because it was popular in country bars. But the count was the same, and she was as light on her feet as he was, so they moved easily around the dance floor.

"I didn't know you could dance so well," she said.

"There are lots of things you don't know about me."

"I'd like to learn."

Burr took a deep breath and let it out. "There's no time like the present, is there? Let me introduce myself. My name is Burr Covington. I'm a Texas Ranger. I grew up in Houston, but I've been assigned to the office in Austin for the past two years."

"It's nice to meet you, Mr. Covington," Lindsey said with a shy smile.

"Please call me Burr."

"I'd be pleased to…Burr. My name is Lindsey Major. People claim I have the bluest eyes in Texas, but they're greatly mistaken. They aren't blue at all. They're—"

"Lavender," Burr finished for her. "And what have you been doing to keep yourself busy these past few weeks, Miss Major?"

"Oh, please, call me…Blue Eyes."

"Well, Blue Eyes?" Burr said, a tender smile teasing his lips.

"I've been talking to my father about going back to college. I never finished my degree in journalism, you know. I've decided to return to Baylor in the fall."

"Then you can be the one to do the writing, instead of being written about."

"That thought has crossed my mind," she said with a mischievous smile.

"I just might be transferring to that area of Texas," Burr said.

"As a Texas Ranger?"

"Yeah. One of my rewards for saving the governor's daughter was my choice of assignments. And I got a raise. So I was thinking about settling down and finding me a wife."

"Oh?"

"Would you by any chance be interested in the job?"

"Why, I think I might be willing to consider such a position. So long as you don't mind getting up every morning to the bluest eyes in Texas."

"No," Burr said as he pulled her close and lowered his mouth to hers. "I don't think I'll mind that at all."